A Reality TV Romance

Michael Gordon

Published by MG Books, 2025.

A REALITY TV ROMANCE

First edition. June 3, 2025.

ISBN: 979-8231025107

Written by Michael Gordon.

Table of Contents

Chapter 1

The sun hung high in the Hawaiian sky, its golden rays piercing through the swaying palm fronds and dappling the grounds of the Love Oasis villa. The air was thick with the scent of plumeria and the distant tang of saltwater, a symphony of nature that welcomed the five women as they stepped onto the marble pathway leading to their temporary home. Claire, Sammy, Katie, Victoria, and Yolanda, each in their bikinis, their laughter mingling with the rustle of tropical foliage, felt the weight of anticipation settle over them. This was it—the beginning of their journey on a reality show that promised love, drama, and self-discovery.

Claire, her slim figure accentuated by a simple black string bikini, her long, straight black hair cascading down her back, paused to take in the grandeur of the villa. Her beige skin glistened with a light sheen of sweat, and her bright smile faltered just a touch as she whispered, "This is so surreal. I mean, look at this place. It's like something out of a dream." Her brown eyes scanned the opulent surroundings—the infinity pool that seemed to merge with the ocean, the lush gardens, the whitewashed walls adorned with vibrant bougainvillea. It was breathtaking, but her nerves were undeniable.

Sammy, her curvy figure showcased in a bold, floral-print bikini top and matching string thong bottoms, placed a reassuring hand on Claire's shoulder. Her olive skin glowed in the sunlight, and her long dark hair, styled in loose waves, framed her vibrant smile. "You'll be fine, Claire," she said, her voice warm and steady. "Just be yourself. That's what's going to make you stand out." Sammy's confidence was infectious, a byproduct of her bold and playful personality, but even she felt a flutter of excitement as she took in the villa.

Katie, her blonde hair shimmering like spun gold in the sunlight, her bright blue eyes sparkling with curiosity, wandered toward the pool. Her fair skin, dusted with freckles across her nose and cheeks, seemed to glow against the vibrant backdrop. Her hourglass figure, accentuated by a high-waisted bikini, turned heads as she moved. "Y'all, this is just like somethin' outta a movie," she drawled, her thick Southern accent as unmistakable as her beauty mark just above her lip. "I can't believe we're actually here."

Victoria, her bronzed skin gleaming as if she'd just stepped off a runway, her enhanced figure on full display in a barely-there metallic bikini, struck a pose by the pool's edge. Her long brunette hair cascaded down her back, and her flawless makeup seemed untouched by the humidity. "This is going to be epic," she declared, her voice dripping with confidence. "I can already feel it. My Instagram followers are going to go wild." Victoria's every move was calculated, her image as a bombshell carefully maintained, but even she couldn't deny the thrill of the moment.

Yolanda, her curvy figure accentuated by a tight-fitting leopard-print bikini, her wavy black hair flowing down her back, leaned against a palm tree, her smoky eyes scanning the villa. Her dark skin was radiant, and her bold lips curved into a mischievous smile. The beauty mark above her left eyebrow added a touch of uniqueness to her striking features. "This place is something else," she murmured, her voice sultry and low. "I can't wait to see what the guys are like."

The women gathered near the pool, drinks in hand, the clinking of ice cubes against glass mingling with their laughter. The conversation turned naturally to what they were looking for in a man, each woman's desires as distinct as their personalities.

Sammy, her voice laced with enthusiasm, spoke first. "I want someone who's down to earth, you know? Someone who can keep up with my energy but also knows how to chill. I'm not here for drama—I'm here for something real." She took a sip of her piña colada, her eyes scanning the horizon as if she could already see her ideal man walking toward her.

Claire, her voice soft but steady, nodded. "I'm looking for someone who's kind and patient. Someone who can make me feel comfortable being myself. I've always been a bit shy, so I need someone who can draw me out of my shell." She twirled a strand of her black hair around her finger, her nerves momentarily forgotten in the warmth of the group.

Katie, her eyes dreamy, chimed in. "I want a real country boy. Someone who knows how to treat a lady, who's not afraid to get his hands dirty. Y'all know I'm from a small town, and I miss that kind of simplicity. Someone who'd fit right in at a Sunday barbecue."

Victoria, her tone confident, added, "I'm here for love, but let's be real, I'm also here to boost my brand. I need someone who's not intimidated by my success. Someone who can stand beside me, not behind me." She adjusted her bikini top, her movements deliberate, as if she were posing for the cameras recording them.

Yolanda, her voice sultry, smiled. "I'm looking for someone who can keep up with me. Someone who's not afraid of a little adventure. I'm not here to settle—I want someone who can match my energy and my ambition."

As they continued to talk, a faint noise echoed in the distance. The women froze, their eyes widening with anticipation. "Do you hear that?" Sammy whispered, her heart racing. "It sounds like... the guys."

The sound grew louder, a mix of laughter and footsteps. The women scrambled to their feet, their excitement palpable. "They're here!" Katie squealed, her Southern accent more pronounced in her excitement. "Y'all, they're actually here!"

Sammy, her nerves tingling, took a deep breath as she watch the girls squeal with excitement. She closed her eyes and under her breath she said, "I hope I can find the man of my dreams. Someone who's not just here for the cameras, but for something real."

Inside the villa, the men were equally aware of the women's presence. Matthew, his tall, lanky frame was shirtless, his swim trunks showcasing his athletic build, whistled as he looked around. His light brown skin glistened with a sheen of sweat, and his shaggy curly hair bounced as he moved, and a scruffy beard covered his cheeks. "Well, I ain't in Snow Hill anymore," he drawled, his deep southern accent thick.

Travis, his muscular frame on full display, his tattoos glinting in the sunlight, laughed. "When did you figure that out, Matthew? For a black guy, you sure act like a country white guy." His slicked-back black hair and gold chain necklace gave him an air of casual confidence.

Matthew rolled his eyes, his freckles standing out against his skin. "I'm mixed, Travis." He sneered. Charging the subject, he asked, "Y'all ain't worried about sharing a bed?"

With his sandy blond hair messy, his tattoos including a large Georgia state outline on his bicep, Will chuckled. "That's a good thing, Matthew," Will said, his voice laced with amusement. "You'll get used to it."

Xavier, his dark skin adorned with intricate tattoos, his closely shaved head gleaming, leaned against the kitchen counter. "Let's not forget why we're here, gentlemen. Love, or something like it." His piercing brown eyes seemed to see right through the others, his tone wry but not unkind.

Zack, his tall, muscular build accentuated by his swim trunks, his short Afro and neatly trimmed goatee giving him a distinguished air, nodded. "Exactly. Let's keep it real and see where this takes us."

As the men explored the villa, they stopped in the kitchen, where several drinks had been prepared for them. Matthew, his curly hair bouncing as he moved, sipped his drink and turned to the others. "So, what are y'all looking for in a woman?"

Travis, his voice confident, spoke first. "I want a blonde or brunette woman who's down to fuck. Someone who knows how to have a good time. No drama, just fun." He grinned, his gold chain catching the light.

Will, his tone carefree, added, "I'm looking for someone who can keep up with me. Someone who's not afraid of a little competition. I'm here to win, and I want a partner who feels the same."

Matthew, his voice thoughtful, chimed in. "I'm looking for a down-to-earth woman. Someone who's not afraid to get her hands dirty, but preferably a tall blonde. I've always had a thing for blondes."

Xavier, his tone dry, raised an eyebrow. "Tall blondes, huh? Sounds like you've got a type, Matthew."

Zack, his voice steady, added, "I'm looking for someone who's real. Someone who's not just here for the cameras or the fame. I want a connection that goes deeper than that."

As they continued to talk, the sound of giggling from the poolside reached their ears. Will, with his eyes lighting up, grinned. "What are we waiting for? Let's go introduce ourselves."

Matthew, his heart racing, followed the men out, his eyes scanning the poolside quietly he prayed, "I hope I can find my true love here. Someone who sees me for who I am, not just my mixed-race identity."

As the men approached the pool, the women's hearts raced with anticipation. Sammy, her nerves tingling, took a deep breath. "Here we go," she whispered, her eyes locking with Matthew's.

The air crackled with tension as the men and women met for the first time. Matthew's eyes immediately landed on Katie, her blonde hair and Southern charm drawing him in. Travis, true to his word, zeroed in on Victoria, his boldness matching her confidence. Will's gaze flickered between Sammy and Yolanda, drawn to their energy and charisma. Xavier, ever the observer, took in the scene, his expression unreadable. Zack, his presence commanding, seemed to notice every detail, his eyes lingering on Claire's shy smile.

The introductions were a whirlwind of laughter, nervous energy, and subtle flirtation. The villa, with its luxurious amenities and sensual atmosphere, seemed to hold its breath, waiting to see what connections would form, what hearts would be broken, and what love stories would unfold.

As the sun began to set, casting a golden glow over the villa, the stage was set for a summer of romance, drama, and self-discovery. The journey had only just begun, and already, the possibilities seemed endless. The sound of waves crashing against the shore mingled with the murmur of conversations, the clinking of glasses, and the occasional burst of laughter. Love Oasis was no longer just a villa—it was a crucible for dreams, desires, and destinies. And as the stars began to twinkle in the deepening blue sky, each person there knew that their lives would never be the same.

Chapter 2

The evening air was thick with anticipation as the contestants of Hot Island gathered around the pool, their eyes gleaming with a mix of excitement and nervousness. The villa's lush gardens, illuminated by string lights, created a magical atmosphere, but the tension was palpable. Each contestant stood in a semi-circle, their silhouettes framed by the soft glow of lanterns hanging from the nearby palm trees. The scent of tropical flowers mingled with the salty breeze from the ocean, heightening the senses of everyone present.

Raven Castaway, the host, stood on a small stage at the center of the gathering, her platinum blonde hair cascading over her shoulders in loose waves. Her sundress, a vibrant coral hue, hugged her slender figure, accentuating her cleavage and long legs. She exuded an air of elegance and provocation, her British accent cutting through the hum of conversation like a knife through silk. Her piercing blue eyes scanned the crowd, locking onto each contestant in turn, as if sizing them up for the journey ahead.

"Welcome, everyone, to Hot Island," Raven began, her voice smooth and commanding, yet laced with a hint of mischief. The contestants fell silent, their attention fully on her. "For the next three weeks, you'll be competing for a chance to win $250,000. But there's a catch—you'll only win if America falls in love with your couple. So, choose wisely, because your decisions tonight will shape your journey."

A murmur rippled through the group, some exchanging glances, others staring intently at the ground. Victoria Chance, her bronzed skin glowing under the lights, leaned closer to Claire Song, her whisper carrying a hint of excitement. "This is it. The moment we've all been waiting for." Claire, her slim frame wrapped in a string bikini, nodded, her brown eyes wide with anticipation.

Raven continued, her tone playful yet firm. "To start, the men will stand on these platforms, and the women will choose their partners.

Remember, if multiple women choose the same man, he'll have the final say. And once you're coupled up, you're locked in—until three days from now, when you'll have the chance to swap. But be warned: America will be watching, and they'll decide who stays and who goes."

The men—Matthew, Travis, Will, Xavier, and Zack—stepped onto their designated platforms, each one trying to appear casual yet confident. Matthew, with his lanky frame, curly hair and scruffy beard, fidgeted slightly, his light brown skin glistening under the lights. His southern accent was thick as he introduced himself, his voice carrying a hint of nervousness. "I'm Matthew, from North Carolina and I'm here to find someone to settle down with. I'm looking for a woman who appreciates the simple things in life."

Travis, his deep tan and slicked-back hair making him stand out, smirked as he took his place. "I'm Travis. I'm here for a good time, not a long time. If you're looking for someone who knows how to have fun, I'm your guy." His gold chain necklace glinted in the light, and his flip-flops slapped against the platform as he shifted his weight.

Will, his sandy blond hair messy and charming, grinned as he addressed the women. "Will here. I'm all about living life to the fullest. If you're ready for an adventure, let's make some memories together." His tattoos, including the large Georgia state outline on his bicep, seemed to pulse with his confidence.

Xavier, his dark skin and intricate tattoos commanding attention, spoke with a confident smile. "Xavier. I'm competitive, but I'm also a romantic at heart. If you're looking for someone who'll fight for you, I'm your man." His closely shaved head gleamed under the lights, and his piercing brown eyes seemed to dare the women to choose him.

Zack, his muscular build and short Afro making him impossible to miss, chuckled as he took his place. "Zack. I'm here to find a real connection. I'm a gym instructor, and I'm looking for someone who's as passionate about life as I am." His multiple tattoos, covering his arms and chest, seemed to tell stories of his own journey.

Raven turned to the women, her gaze sweeping over them like a queen surveying her court. "Ladies, it's your turn. Choose wisely."

Claire, her long black hair and shy smile, stepped forward first. She hesitated, her eyes darting between the men, her hands clasping and unclasping nervously. "I... I'll choose Zack. He seems nice, and I like that he's passionate about fitness."

Zack's face lit up with a warm smile, his dimples deepening. "Thanks, Claire. I'm looking forward to getting to know you."

Sammy Rodriguez, her bold personality shining through, strode forward without hesitation. Her tiny bikini top and string thong bottoms left little to the imagination, and her vibrant smile was impossible to ignore. "Matthew. I've always had a thing for country boys, and his accent is just... chef's kiss. It reminds me of Texas."

Matthew's eyes widened, a mix of surprise and apprehension crossing his face. "Uh... thanks, Sammy. I'll do my best to look past... well, everything."

"Everything?" Sammy asked.

"You seem to be on the younger side... and short... I don't usually date women younger and shorter than me."

Sammy rolled her eyes, but there was a hint of annoyance in her voice. "Jeez, didn't even give me a chance."

Raven intervened, her tone light but firm. "Matthew, I appreciate your honesty, but remember, this is about more than just looks. Give it a chance."

Matthew nodded, his expression softening. "You're right. I'll try. I'm sorry Sammy."

"It's cool..." she mumbled, crossing her arms.

Victoria, her confidence radiating from every pore, sauntered forward, her enhanced breasts and long legs turning heads. "Xavier. He's got that bad-boy charm, and I'm here for it."

Xavier's smile was predatory, his gaze locking onto Victoria's. "Looking forward to it, Victoria."

Yolanda Smith, her curves accentuated by her animal print bikini, chose Will. "Will seems like he knows how to have a good time, and that's exactly what I'm looking for."

Will's grin was infectious, his sandy blond hair catching the light. "Let's make this summer unforgettable, Yolanda."

Katie Light, her southern accent thick and her smile warm, hesitated before choosing Travis. "Travis seems like he's got a lot of energy, and I'm ready for some fun."

Travis smirked, his gaze lingering on Katie's hourglass figure. "Let's see if we can keep up with each other."

Once the couples were formed, Raven clapped her hands, her expression satisfied. "Remember, these couples aren't permanent. In three days, you'll have the chance to swap. Until then, get to know your partners, and get a good night's rest. Tomorrow, we'll test your compatibility, and the real fun begins."

As the contestants dispersed, the villa buzzed with conversation. Claire and Zack found themselves sitting by the pool, the water reflecting the twinkling lights above. Claire's shyness was evident, her hands twisting in her lap as she avoided eye contact.

"So... what do you like to do for fun?" Zack asked, his tone gentle, his muscular arms resting casually on his thighs.

Claire laughed nervously, her long black hair falling over her shoulders. "I... I like anime, actually. And Korean dramas. It's kind of embarrassing."

Zack's eyes lit up, his smile genuine. "No way! I'm a huge anime fan too. What's your favorite?"

Claire's face brightened, her shyness melting away. "My Hero Academia. What about you?"

"Same! I love the action and the characters. It's so well done."

As they talked, Claire's nervousness began to fade, replaced by a sense of ease. Zack's genuine interest and shared passion made her feel comfortable, and for the first time since arriving, she felt a glimmer of hope that this might work.

Meanwhile, Sammy and Matthew sat on a nearby lounge chair, the tension between them palpable. Sammy's bold personality clashed with Matthew's reserved nature, and their conversation was stilted.

"So... you're a farmer, huh?" Sammy asked, her tone teasing, her olive skin glowing under the lights.

Matthew nodded, his expression cautious, his freckles standing out against his light brown skin. "Yeah. It's a simple life, but it's all I've ever known."

Sammy rolled her eyes, her distinctive beauty mark above her left eyebrow accentuating her expression. "Simple? Sounds boring. I'm more of a city girl myself."

Matthew chuckled, a hint of dryness in his voice. "I can tell. But hey, maybe I can show you a different side of life."

Sammy's expression softened slightly, her vibrant smile returning. "Maybe. But you'll have to keep up with me."

Across the villa, Victoria and Xavier stood by the bar, their chemistry electric. Victoria's revealing outfit and Xavier's shirtless physique drew glances from everyone around them.

"So, what's your story, Xavier?" Victoria asked, her voice low and flirtatious.

Xavier leaned closer, his piercing brown eyes locking onto hers. "My story? Let's just say I've always been a fighter. And I'm not afraid to go after what I want."

Victoria smirked, her confidence unwavering. "I like that. I'm not one to back down either."

Their flirting was effortless, their connection immediate. It was clear to everyone watching that they were a force to be reckoned with.

Yolanda and Will found themselves by the outdoor bar, their conversation revolving around parties and fun. Yolanda's tight-fitting dress and Will's casual charm made them an attractive pair, but their connection felt more superficial.

"So, Will, what's the craziest thing you've ever done?" Yolanda asked, her long wavy hair cascading over her shoulders.

Will grinned, his tattoos seeming to glow under the lights. "Oh, you know, the usual—skydiving, road trips, spontaneous trips to Vegas. What about you?"

Yolanda laughed, her bold lips curving into a smile. "I once went to a music festival in another country just because my favorite DJ was playing. No plans, just showed up."

Their laughter echoed through the villa, but beneath the surface, it was clear they were still strangers, their connection based more on shared interests than deep understanding.

Katie and Travis, despite their initial attraction, struggled to find common ground. They sat on a bench overlooking the ocean, the waves crashing against the shore in the distance.

"So, Katie, what do you do back home?" Travis asked, his tone casual, his deep tan making him look like he belonged on the beach.

Katie's warm smile faltered slightly, her southern accent thick as she replied. "I'm a nurse. It's rewarding, but it can be tough."

Travis nodded, his expression thoughtful. "That's admirable. I'm more of a free spirit. I work as a surf instructor, so I'm always on the move."

Katie's bright blue eyes flickered with uncertainty. "That sounds fun, but I'm more of a homebody. I like routine."

Their differences became more apparent with each passing minute, the silence between them growing heavier. It was clear they were on different wavelengths, their initial attraction fading as reality set in.

In the background, Raven watched it all unfold, a small smile playing on her lips. She knew that the real drama was yet to come, and she couldn't wait to see how these couples would navigate the challenges ahead. As the contestants got to know each other more, the villa felt alive with energy as each person wanted to know more about the person they are dating.

As the evening went on, the currents of desire, doubt, and anticipation swirled, setting the stage for a summer that would change their lives forever. The night deepened, and the villa's magical atmosphere seemed to hold its breath, waiting for the storm of emotions that was sure to come.

Chapter 3

As the moon shined on the horizon, Sammy Rodriguez and Matthew Brown made their way from the bustling kitchen of the Love Oasis villa. Their drinks in hand—Sammy's a fruity cocktail with a tiny umbrella, Matthew's a simple beer—they moved away from the laughter and chatter of the other contestants. The villa, with its whitewashed walls and terracotta tiles, seemed to glow in the nightlight, the air thick with the scent of blooming jasmine and the distant saltiness of the ocean.

They settled into a pair of lounge chairs by the pool, the water's surface shimmering from the moonlight. Sammy, dipped her toes into the cool water, splashing softly. Matthew followed suit, his long legs stretching out as he leaned back, his light brown skin glinting with a sheen of sweat from the island's heat. The silence between them was comfortable at first, the kind that comes with the ease of shared space, but it soon stretched into something awkward, broken only by the distant hum of cicadas and the occasional laugh from the villa's courtyard.

Sammy took a sip of her drink, the sweetness of mango and pineapple lingering on her lips. She glanced at Matthew, his tall, lanky frame relaxed yet somehow tense, as if he were still adjusting to the unfamiliarity of it all. His curly hair, a mess of tight ringlets, caught the light, and she noticed the freckles scattered across his nose and cheeks, a detail she hadn't taken in before.

"So," Matthew finally said, his deep southern accent breaking the silence, "I really am sorry about earlier. I didn't mean to come off like that."

Sammy shrugged, her long dark hair falling over her shoulder as she turned to face him. "It's cool. We're all here to figure things out, right? No hard feelings."

He nodded, his expression softening. "I guess I'm just not used to… this. Being around so many people, you know? Back home, it's just me, the farm, and the horses."

"Horses, huh?" Sammy smiled, her vibrant grin lighting up her face. The beauty mark above her left eyebrow seemed to dance with her expression. "That sounds nice. I've always wanted to ride one. I'm more of a city girl, though. Houston's my home."

Matthew chuckled, a warm sound that eased the tension further. "Houston, yeah? That's a big change from Snow Hill. I mean, we don't even have a stoplight in my town."

Sammy laughed, the sound bubbling up from her chest. "I can't imagine that. I'm used to traffic and noise. But I guess it's nice to have a break from all that."

They lapsed into another silence, but this time it felt less heavy, more natural. Sammy swirled her drink, watching the ice cubes clink against the glass. The tiny umbrella bobbed with each movement, a whimsical touch that made her smile. "So, you said you've only dated taller women. What's up with that?"

Matthew's cheeks flushed slightly, and he scratched the back of his neck, a gesture that seemed both nervous and endearing. "I don't know. It's just… what I'm used to, I guess. But you're right, short women can be fun too."

"Fun?" Sammy raised an eyebrow, her tone playful. "I'm not just fun, Matthew. I'm a whole experience. And if you're worried about height, I can always find a box to stand on to kiss you."

His grin was immediate, his dimples deepening as his eyes crinkled at the corners. "You're already talking about kissing me? You move fast, Sammy Rodriguez."

"Hey, a girl's gotta keep her options open," she teased, her laughter bubbling up again. "Besides, you're the one who brought it up."

The tension between them eased as they fell into an easy banter, their differences seeming less like barriers and more like bridges.

Matthew told her more about his family farm, his hands gesturing animatedly as he described the sprawling cornfields, the clucking chickens, and the way the sun rose over the pastures. Sammy listened intently, her curiosity piqued. "I can't imagine waking up to that every day. I'm more of a brunch-and-mimosas kind of girl."

"Well, maybe I can show you what you're missing," he said, his voice warm. "I ride horses all the time. You'd love it."

Sammy's eyes widened, her expression a mix of surprise and delight. "You ride horses? For real? That sounds amazing. I've always wanted to try it."

"Definitely," he said, his smile softening. "Maybe one day I'll take you."

The conversation flowed naturally from there, their differences weaving together like threads in a tapestry. Sammy told him about her time as a cheerleader in college, her voice tinged with nostalgia. "Now that I'm out, I don't really know what to do. I thought about teaching Spanish to kids. What do you think?"

Matthew's eyes lit up, his entire demeanor shifting with excitement. "That's awesome. I speak Spanish too. A lot of the farm hands do, so I picked it up."

"No way!" Sammy grinned, her eyes sparkling with challenge. "Prove it."

Without hesitation, Matthew switched to fluent Spanish, his accent smooth and natural. "¿Cómo estás, Sammy? ¿Te gusta la vida en la isla?"

She giggled, responding in kind. "Estoy bien, gracias. La isla es hermosa, pero extrañaré la ciudad."

He laughed, clearly impressed. "You're good. I didn't expect that."

"What can I say? I'm full of surprises," she said, her grin widening. "You're something else, Matthew Brown."

"You're something else too," he replied, his tone gentle, his gaze holding hers for a moment longer than necessary.

The night deepened around them, the stars beginning to peek through the darkening sky. The villa felt quieter now, the other contestants having retreated to their rooms or the love suite. The pool's water had stilled, reflecting the twinkling lights of the villa like a mirror. Sammy and Matthew sat in comfortable silence for a moment, their drinks long forgotten on the edge of the pool.

"So, what's your plan here?" Matthew asked, breaking the quiet. "I mean, besides finding a box to kiss me on."

Sammy laughed, her shoulders lifting in a shrug. Her string bikini clung to her curves as she moved. "Honestly? I don't know. I'm just trying to figure it out. Maybe I'll teach Spanish, maybe I'll travel. Who knows?"

"Sounds like you've got options," he said, his voice steady. "But whatever you choose, I'm sure you'll be great at it."

She smiled, her heart warming at his words. "Thanks, Matthew. That means a lot."

The moment stretched between them, charged with unspoken possibilities. Sammy felt a flutter in her chest, a mix of excitement and nervousness. She glanced at him, her eyes meeting his, and for a second, she wondered if he felt it too. His gaze was intense, his expression unreadable, before he looked away, clearing his throat.

"We should probably head in," he said, standing and stretching his long limbs. "It's getting late."

Sammy nodded, standing as well. Her bikini hugged her curves as she moved, and she adjusted her bikini top, suddenly self-conscious. "Yeah, I guess so."

They walked back to their shared room in silence, the weight of the evening hanging between them. The villa's corridors were dimly lit, the air cool after the warmth of the night. The room felt smaller than before, the queen-sized bed dominating the space. Sammy hesitated, then spoke up. "I'll take the shower first, if that's okay."

"Sure," Matthew said, his voice neutral. "Take your time."

She grabbed her toiletries and headed into the bathroom, the door clicking shut behind her. The shower was a welcome respite, the warm water washing away the day's tension. She let her mind wander back to the conversation by the pool, replaying Matthew's laughter, his Spanish, the way his eyes had held hers. When she emerged, she wrapped herself in a towel, her hair still damp and curling around her face.

She dressed quickly in a tank top and short shorts, her go-to outfit for comfort. As she stepped out, she caught Matthew's gaze, his eyes lingering on her figure. She felt a flush rise to her cheeks, but she smiled, trying to play it cool.

"You look nice," he said, his voice low.

"Thanks," she replied, her voice soft. "You too."

He nodded, then headed into the bathroom himself. When he emerged, shirtless and wearing only a pair of loose pants, Sammy couldn't help but stare. His lean, muscular build was impressive, the small patch of chest hair adding a rugged charm. She looked away quickly, feeling her cheeks heat up.

They stood awkwardly for a moment, the silence thick between them. Finally, Matthew spoke. "We should probably get some sleep. Big day tomorrow."

Sammy nodded, her heart pounding. "Yeah, goodnight, Matthew."

"Goodnight, Sammy," he replied, his voice gentle.

They climbed into the bed, the space between them feeling both vast and impossibly small. Sammy lay on her side, her back to Matthew, her mind racing. She could feel his presence, the warmth of his body just inches away. Part of her wanted to reach out, to bridge the gap between them, but she held back, unsure of how he'd react.

Matthew shifted in the bed, his movements careful. She wondered if he was feeling the same way, if he was debating whether to make a move. But the moments stretched on, and neither of them spoke.

Eventually, the villa fell silent, the only sound the distant hum of the ocean. Sammy closed her eyes, her thoughts a jumble of the evening's conversation, the warmth of Matthew's smile, and the unspoken tension between them. She wondered what the next day would bring, if they'd pick up where they left off or if the moment would fade into the background of their time on the island.

As sleep finally claimed her, Sammy couldn't shake the feeling that something had shifted between them, a connection forming in the quiet moments by the pool and the awkward silence of their shared bed. But whether it would grow into something more, only time would tell.

The night deepened, the villa quiet and still, as two strangers lay side by side, their hearts beating in rhythm, their futures uncertain but intertwined.

Chapter 4

The morning sun bathed the Love Oasis villa in a warm, golden light, its rays filtering through the palm fronds and dappling the pool's surface. Inside the makeup room, the air was thick with the scent of coconut sunscreen, mingling with the faint aroma of freshly brewed coffee and the sweet tang of lip gloss. Sammy Rodriguez sat in her makeup chair, her olive skin glowing under the soft lighting, as she delicately sipped her coffee. Her tiny string bikini, a bold shade of turquoise, accentuated her curvy figure, while her long dark hair cascaded in loose waves over her shoulders. The distinctive beauty mark above her left eyebrow seemed to sparkle with her every movement.

Around her, the other women lounged in their chairs, their conversations a mix of laughter, whispered secrets, and the occasional sigh. Claire Song, her slim frame draped in a black string bikini, sat nearby, her long black hair falling straight down her back. Her bright smile was absent this morning, replaced by a thoughtful expression as she watched Sammy savor her coffee. Claire could tell she was deep in thought about Matthew.

"You have a good man," Claire remarked softly, her voice gentle but filled with admiration. Her brown eyes held a knowing glint, as if she could see the turmoil beneath Sammy's vibrant smile.

Sammy paused, her fork hovering midway to her lips. "I know, but there's still this doubt, you know? Like, is it too good to be true?" She glanced at the other women, her expression a mix of gratitude and uncertainty. "He's so sweet, but I can't shake the feeling that there's something I'm missing."

Yolanda Smith, her curvy figure accentuated by a tight-fitting leopard-print bikini, leaned forward, her smoky eyes narrowing thoughtfully. Her long, wavy black hair cascaded over her shoulders, and her bold red lips curved into a mischievous smile. "Girl, you're overthinking it. Matthew's a catch. He's cute and, he's sweet. That's more than most guys around here would do." She paused, her voice dropping to a conspiratorial whisper. "Besides, have you seen the way he looks at you? He's into you, Sammy. Don't let your insecurities get in the way."

Katie Light, her blonde hair cascading in loose waves over her shoulders, remained silent, her blue eyes fixed intently on her makeup palette as she aggressively applied her eyeliner. Her fair skin, dusted with freckles, seemed to glow under the soft lighting, but her expression was tight, her jaw clenched. She had been paired with Travis, but their connection seemed strained, and her focus was clearly elsewhere.

Victoria Chance, her enhanced breasts and long, toned legs on full display in a metallic gold bikini, chimed in, her confident voice filling the room. "Yolanda's right. Matthew's a keeper. But you know what they say, Sammy—trust your instincts. If something feels off, it probably is." She adjusted her bikini top, her bronzed skin glistening under the lights, and shot Sammy a knowing look. "But don't let doubt ruin a good thing. You two have chemistry, and that's rare in this place."

Sammy nodded, her long dark hair swaying with the movement. "I know. It's just...he brought up the age difference, the height. Those seemed to be like dealbreakers for him. It's like, is he really into me, or is he just settling?" She took another sip of her coffee, her thoughts swirling like the steam rising from her coffee cup.

Claire's gentle voice broke the tension. "Sometimes, the best relationships are the ones we don't see coming. Maybe Matthew's exactly what you need, Sammy. Someone different, someone who challenges you in a good way." Her words were soft but carried a weight of wisdom, as if she had experienced similar doubts herself.

As the women continued their conversation, the door to the makeup room swung open, and Matthew Brown stood in the doorway, a plate of Huevos Rancheros in his hands. His tall, lanky frame was shirtless, his swim trunks clinging to his athletic build. His curly hair was tousled, and his deep southern accent was warm and reassuring. A faint sheen of sweat glistened on his light brown skin, evidence of warm island weather.

"Sorry to interrupt, ladies, but I made breakfast for Sammy," he said, his voice filled with genuine care. "Hope you don't mind me crashing the party."

Sammy's eyes widened in surprise, and a blush crept up her cheeks, warming her olive skin. "Really? You made this for me?"

Matthew grinned, his freckles standing out against his skin. "Yeah, the guys were busy, and I figured you probably hadn't eaten yet. I hope you like Huevos Rancheros."

"I do," Sammy replied, her voice soft but filled with gratitude. "Thank you, Matthew. This means a lot."

He smiled, his eyes crinkling at the corners, and handed her the plate. "No problem. See you out there," he said, nodding to the other women before leaving the room. The scent of his cologne, a hint of sandalwood and citrus, lingered briefly in the air.

The women exchanged glances, their expressions a mix of envy and admiration. "Damn, Sammy," Yolanda said, her voice laced with jealousy. "He's a keeper. Don't let him go."

Katie finally spoke up, her voice sharp and dismissive as she smudged her eyeliner with a cotton swab. "He's nice, but let's not forget he said that you're not really his type."

Sammy frowned, her fork pausing midway to her mouth. "What's that supposed to mean, Katie?"

Katie shrugged, her blonde hair falling over her shoulders. "Just saying, he said he always gone for taller girls. Matthew's great, but aren't you worried he'd try to swap for a different women?"

Sammy's frown deepened, her thoughts turning inward. "Maybe, but I have to try, right?" She took another bite of her breakfast, her gaze drifting toward the window, where the villa's lush gardens were bathed in morning light. As she sat there eating Katie's question lingered in her brain.

Outside, the villa buzzed with activity. The guys, shirtless and sweaty, were working out by the pool, their muscles glistening under the Hawaiian sun. Will Wright, his sandy blond hair messy and his tattoos on full display, paused mid-rep to check out Yolanda from a distance. His chiseled jawline tightened as he lifted weights, his gaze lingering on her curvy dark skinned figure.

"Damn, the crew at Hot Island sure knows how to pick them," he said, setting down his dumbbells with a clatter. His voice was filled with admiration, his Georgia state tattoo on his bicep flexing with the movement. "Yolanda's got curves for days. I love a woman with a figure like that."

Travis Russo, his deep tan and slicked-back black hair making him stand out, bragged about his night with Katie. "She's a firecracker, that one. We had a great time last night," he said, his gold chain necklace glinting in the sunlight. His voice carried a hint of smugness, as if he were reliving the moment.

Zack Gardner, his muscular build and short Afro making him a commanding presence, turned to Matthew, who was taking a water break. "So, how was your night with Sammy? Anything happen?" His voice was casual, but his eyes held a curious glint, as if he were probing for details.

Matthew shrugged, his expression thoughtful as he wiped his forehead with a towel. "We talked all night. It was nice, but..." He trailed off, his eyes drifting toward Sammy, who was now lounging by the pool with Yolanda. Her curvy figure was on full display as she lay on her stomach, her tiny bikini leaving little to the imagination. Her laughter carried across the pool, light and infectious.

Will followed Matthew's gaze and let out a low whistle, his eyes widening appreciatively. "Damn, brother. Look at that ass. You're telling me you're not feeling her? That's a definition of a bubble butt right there. I'd be getting hard just looking at it."

Matthew's eyes narrowed, his expression conflicted. "It's not that simple, Will. She's shorter than me, and she's younger. It feels like I'm dating my sister's friends. It's... weird." His voice carried a hint of frustration, as if he were wrestling with his own thoughts.

Zack laughed, his deep voice filling the air. "Brother, you're overthinking it. Look at her. She's gorgeous, and she's into you. Don't let something like height stop you from going after what you want." He clapped Matthew on the shoulder, his expression encouraging.

Matthew's gaze lingered on Sammy, his thoughts swirling like the leaves in the gentle breeze. He had come to the show looking for a wife, someone to bring home to his parents and build a future with. But Sammy was different. She was vibrant, confident, and unlike anyone he had ever dated. The age difference and height disparity had initially bothered him, but as he spent more time with her, he found himself drawn to her energy and spirit.

Xavier's voice broke through his thoughts, his tone teasing but with an edge of seriousness. "If you're not feeling her, I might have to make a move. I'd hate to see all that ass go to waste."

Matthew's expression hardened, a protective instinct rising within him. "She's mine, Xavier. I'm not giving her up." His voice was firm, his southern accent more pronounced as his resolve strengthened.

Zack clapped Matthew on the back, his smile wide and genuine. "That's what I like to hear. Go after what you want, brother. Don't let doubt hold you back."

As the guys continued their workout, Matthew's gaze remained fixed on Sammy. The sun glinted off the pool's surface, casting shimmering reflections on the surrounding tiles. He knew the road ahead wouldn't be easy. There would be challenges, doubts, and obstacles to overcome. But in that moment, as he watched her laugh with Yolanda, her vibrant smile lighting up the villa, he felt a surge of determination. He wanted to get to know her, to explore the connection they shared. And he was willing to do whatever it took to make it work.

The villa buzzed with energy as the contestants prepared for the day ahead. The sun shone brightly, the pool sparkled, and the air was filled with the promise of new beginnings. For Matthew and Sammy, the journey was just beginning, and the possibilities were endless.

As Matthew turned away from the pool, his mind was made up. He would give their relationship a chance, no matter the challenges that lay ahead. He hoped he was making the right choice, but one thing was certain—he wasn't ready to let Sammy go. The sound of her laughter echoed in his mind, a melody that he knew he couldn't live without.

Chapter 5

The sun hung low in the Hawaiian sky, painting the horizon in hues of amber and coral as the contestants of Hot Island gathered on the pristine beach for their first couples challenge. The air was thick with anticipation, the salty tang of the ocean mingling with the faint scent of coconut sunscreen and the earthy aroma of the nearby palm trees. Raven Castaway, her platinum blonde hair cascading in loose waves down her back, stood at the center of the group, her low-cut sundress in vibrant fuchsia accentuating her cleavage and long legs. Her piercing blue eyes scanned the crowd, a mix of amusement and calculation flashing across her elegant features.

"Alright, everyone, gather 'round!" Raven's voice carried effortlessly, her British accent lending an air of authority. The contestants, dressed in costumes of neon 80s workout gear, exchanged nervous glances as they huddled closer. The guys, in tight neon short shorts and tank tops, showcased their toned muscles, while the girls, in spandex leotards and leggings, flaunted their curves. Sammy Rodriguez, her olive skin glowing under the sun and her long dark hair tied back in a high ponytail, stood beside Matthew Brown, her partner for the challenge. Matthew, tall and lanky with curly hair, scruffy beard and a light dusting of freckles on his nose, adjusted the neon green shorts he felt slightly ridiculous in.

"Ready when you are, Raven," Matthew called out, his deep southern accent drawing a few smiles from the group. His easy charm was undeniable, but beneath the surface, he felt a twinge of unease. The challenge ahead seemed simple enough, but he knew teamwork wasn't his strongest suit.

"Great! Let's get started," Raven said, clapping her hands. Her strappy sandals glinted in the sunlight as she stepped forward. "Today's challenge is all about teamwork, communication, and trust—three things that are essential in any successful relationship. You'll be competing in a three-legged obstacle course race through this maze. The winning couple will receive a romantic date and immunity from being voted out this week. So, let's see who's truly compatible."

The maze, constructed from bamboo and colorful fabric, loomed ahead, its twists and turns promising both excitement and frustration. The contestants murmured among themselves, some pairing up to strategize while others simply admired the setup. Victoria Chance, her bronzed skin shimmering in a neon orange leotard, whispered something to Xavier Cross, who stood shirtless, his intricate tattoos glinting in the sunlight. Claire Song, in a neon pink ensemble, laughed lightly as she adjusted her leg tie with Zack Gardner, his muscular frame towering beside her.

"Alright, everyone at the sound of the whistle go," Raven announced, her gaze locking onto the pair. "Remember, communication is key. Good luck!"

Sammy and Matthew stepped forward, their legs tied together with a bright pink rope. Sammy's tan cleavage peeked out from under her neon yellow leotard, a bold contrast to Matthew's more subdued neon green shorts.

"Alright, let's do this," Sammy said, her voice cheerful but tinged with nerves. Her distinctive beauty mark above her left eyebrow seemed to glint with determination. "We've got this, right?"

Matthew nodded, his expression determined but his heart racing. "Just follow my lead. We'll take it slow and steady."

The whistle blew, and they were off. At first, their movements were synchronized, their steps falling into a natural rhythm as they navigated the maze's initial turns. The sand beneath their feet was warm, and the ocean breeze carried the distant sound of waves crashing against the shore. But as they approached the first obstacle—a series of hurdles—their coordination began to falter.

"Jump!" Matthew shouted, his voice cutting through the air. But Sammy hesitated, her foot catching on the rope. They stumbled, nearly falling before catching themselves on the bamboo frame.

"We need to talk more," Sammy panted, frustration creeping into her voice. Her olive skin flushed with exertion, and her ponytail swayed as she turned to face him. "You're going too fast."

"I'm trying to keep us moving," Matthew replied, his tone defensive. "We're already behind. Look at the others—they're almost at the next obstacle."

Their voices grew louder as they argued, their movements becoming more disjointed. The rope binding their legs seemed to tighten, as if symbolizing the tension between them. Nearby, Claire and Zack watched with a mix of sympathy and concern.

"They're not doing so well," Claire observed, her voice soft. Her slim frame was clad in a neon pink leotard that matched her bright smile, now faded into a frown.

Zack nodded, his arms crossed over his broad chest. "Communication's a problem. They're not on the same page."

Meanwhile, Sammy and Matthew reached the next obstacle—a series of balance beams. Their lack of coordination became even more apparent as they struggled to stay upright. The beams were narrow, and the rope binding their legs made it difficult to maintain balance.

"Left foot first!" Matthew instructed, but Sammy misheard him and stepped with her right, causing them to wobble dangerously.

"I said left!" Matthew snapped, his patience wearing thin. His southern accent grew more pronounced as his frustration mounted.

"You're not being clear!" Sammy shot back, her voice rising. "Just calm down and explain it properly!"

Their argument drew glances from the other contestants, some smirking, others exchanging sympathetic looks. Yolanda Smith, her curvy figure accentuated by a neon blue leotard, whispered something to Will Wright, who stood shirtless, his sandy blond hair catching the sunlight.

"They're not going to last if they keep this up," Yolanda remarked, her voice laced with concern.

Will nodded, his chiseled jaw set in a grim line. "They need to figure out how to work together or they're done."

By the time Sammy and Matthew finished the course, they were in last place, their faces flushed with frustration and embarrassment. The other couples cheered for the winners—Victoria and Xavier, who had moved with seamless coordination—while Sammy and Matthew stood apart, their shoulders tense.

"We really messed that up," Sammy muttered, her hands on her hips. Her vibrant smile was nowhere to be seen, replaced by a furrowed brow and a tight lip.

Matthew sighed, running a hand through his curly hair. "Yeah, we did. I don't know what happened. We just couldn't get it together."

"Maybe we're not as compatible as we thought," Sammy said, her voice quiet but loaded with doubt. The words hung in the air like a weight, pressing down on both of them.

Matthew's expression darkened. "Is that what you think? That we're not meant to be together?"

"I didn't say that," Sammy replied quickly, but the damage was done. The question lingered, unspoken but felt, a crack in the foundation of their relationship.

Later that night, the villa was alive with activity. Music played softly in the background, a mix of 80s hits and modern pop, while the contestants mingled by the pool. The earlier outfits had been replaced with casual beachwear, but the tension from the challenge still lingered. Sammy sat on one of the lounge chairs, a tropical drink in her hand, her mind replaying the day's events. She noticed Matthew across the pool, laughing with Katie Light, his easy charm on full display. Katie's bright blue eyes sparkled as she leaned in, her blonde hair cascading over her shoulders.

Sammy's chest tightened. She knew Katie had expressed doubts about her and Matthew's compatibility, and seeing them together now only fueled her insecurities. She took a sip of her drink, the sweetness doing little to ease the bitterness in her heart.

"Hey, Sammy," Claire said, sitting down beside her. Her neon pink bikini top and sarong contrasted with her calm demeanor. "You okay? You seem a bit distracted."

Sammy forced a smile, her beauty mark twitching slightly. "Yeah, I'm fine. Just thinking about the challenge earlier. We really bombed it."

Claire nodded sympathetically, her brown eyes warm with understanding. "It's tough when things don't go as planned. But you guys will figure it out. You're both great together."

"I hope so," Sammy murmured, her gaze drifting back to Matthew and Katie. The way they laughed together, the ease in their body language—it all felt like a knife twisting in her chest.

As the night wore on, Matthew remained distant, his earlier enthusiasm replaced by a quiet reserve. Sammy tried to engage him in conversation, but he brushed her off, his attention divided between her and the others.

"Matthew, can we talk?" Sammy asked, her voice low as they stood by the pool's edge. The water rippled softly, reflecting the string lights that hung above.

He hesitated, his eyes flicking toward Katie before returning to Sammy. "Not right now, Sammy. I'm not in the mood."

Hurt flashed across Sammy's face, but she nodded, biting her lip. "Okay. Goodnight, then."

She turned and walked away, her heart heavy. The villa's vibrant atmosphere felt suffocating, the laughter and music grating on her nerves. As she made her way to their shared bedroom, she couldn't shake the feeling that things were slipping away.

In the bedroom, Matthew was already in bed, his back turned to her. Sammy changed into her pajamas, the silence between them thick and uncomfortable. She lay down beside him, staring at the ceiling, her thoughts racing. The fan above them whirred softly, doing little to cool the heat of her emotions.

"Matthew," she began softly, her voice trembling slightly, "I know things have been weird between us. But I want to talk about it. I want to make this work."

He didn't respond, his silence speaking volumes. Sammy sighed, her eyes stinging with unshed tears. She turned to face him, but he remained still, his expression unreadable in the dim light.

"Goodnight," she whispered, her voice breaking.

He mumbled a reply, his back still turned. Sammy closed her eyes, the weight of uncertainty pressing down on her. For the first time since arriving at Love Oasis, she wondered if it was better to let go before things got even more complicated.

Chapter 6

The morning sun bathed the Love Oasis villa in a golden haze, its rays filtering through the palm trees and dappling the pool's turquoise surface. The air was thick with the scent of blooming frangipani and the faint tang of saltwater from the nearby ocean. Inside the open-concept kitchen, the women had gathered around the marble island, their voices rising and falling like the tide as they recounted the events of the previous night. Claire Song, her long, straight black hair cascading over her shoulders, laughed softly as Victoria, described her steamy make-out session with Xavier. Katie, her sun-kissed curls bouncing, giggled as she recounted her own intimate moments with Travis, her hand brushing his arm affectionately.

Sammy Rodriguez, however, sat quietly at the edge of the group, her olive skin flushed with a mix of embarrassment and discomfort. She fiddled with the strap of her tiny bikini top, her vibrant smile absent as the conversation inevitably turned to her. The other women's curious glances felt like a spotlight, and she shifted uncomfortably in her seat.

"So, Sammy, what about you and Matthew?" Claire asked, her brown eyes widening with curiosity. "Did you guys... you know?"

Sammy's cheeks warmed, and she avoided eye contact, staring instead at the coffee in front of her. "Uh, no. Not really." Her voice was barely above a whisper, and she could feel the weight of their stares.

The other women exchanged glances, their expressions a mix of surprise and sympathy. Sammy felt a pang of embarrassment. She hadn't expected the morning to start like this, with everyone dissecting her relationship—or lack thereof—with Matthew. Just as she was about to change the subject, the kitchen door swung open, and Matthew Brown walked in, a tray of fresh fruit, homemade pancakes, and bacon in his hands. His tall, lanky frame moved with an easy grace, and his curly hair was still damp from a morning swim, droplets glistening in the sunlight.

"Morning, ladies," he said, his deep southern accent drawing their attention. He placed the tray in front of Sammy, his gaze lingering on her for a moment before he turned to leave. The warmth of his smile felt like a private moment, but it only added to Sammy's confusion.

"You didn't have to do that," Sammy said quickly, her voice softer than she intended. She appreciated the gesture, but it only highlighted the awkwardness between them.

Matthew paused, his hand on the door handle. "I like to," he replied simply before stepping out. The door clicked shut behind him, leaving Sammy with a mix of frustration and gratitude.

Sammy rolled her eyes, a mix of emotions bubbling inside her. Claire noticed her reaction and leaned closer, her voice dropping to a whisper. "What's up with that?"

Sammy sighed, her fingers tracing the edge of her bikini top. "I don't know. He keeps bringing me breakfast, but we haven't even kissed yet. It's like he's sending mixed signals. I can't figure him out."

Claire nodded thoughtfully, her expression understanding. "Every couple moves at their own pace. But if you're feeling like it's not working, maybe you should think about swapping partners. You know, before it's too late."

Sammy shrugged, her mind racing. She didn't want to give up on Matthew, but she couldn't ignore the growing uncertainty in her chest. The villa's rules were clear: if a couple wasn't progressing, they could request a swap. But the thought of being with someone else felt like admitting defeat.

Later that day, Sammy and Claire lounged by the pool, the sun warming their skin as the men played football on the lawn. The sound of laughter and shouts filled the air, mingling with the distant crash of waves. Claire leaned back on her elbows, her string bikini glistening in the sunlight.

"I love watching them play shirtless," she said with a dreamy sigh. "Look at the way the sweat rolls off Zack's muscles. He's like a Greek god."

Sammy followed her gaze, her eyes landing on Matthew. He stood with Zack, tossing the football back and forth. His lean, athletic build was accentuated by the way his swim trunks clung to his hips. She felt a flutter in her stomach as she watched him laugh, his deep voice carrying across the yard. His scruffy beard and freckles gave him a rugged charm that she found irresistible, yet frustratingly distant.

"Do you think it's weird that Matthew and I haven't kissed yet?" Sammy asked, her voice barely above a whisper. She propped herself up on her elbows, her string thong bikini bottoms digging into her hips as she adjusted her position. "All the other couples have made out, except for us."

Claire tilted her head, considering. "Not necessarily. Like I said, every couple is different. But if you're not feeling it, you shouldn't force it. Maybe you should talk to him about it. Communication is key."

Sammy nodded absently, her eyes still on Matthew. She watched as he caught the football, his movements fluid and confident. Her thoughts were interrupted by the sound of Zack's laughter. He and Matthew were talking, their heads close together as they paused the game. Sammy couldn't hear what they were saying, but she noticed Matthew glance in her direction before nodding. Her heart skipped a beat, but she quickly looked away, pretending to adjust her sunglasses.

"What do you think they're talking about?" she asked Claire, her voice casual despite the tightness in her chest.

Claire shrugged, her attention already drifting back to the game. "Probably just guy stuff. You know how they are."

Sammy turned onto her stomach, her curvy figure on full display as she rested her chin on her hands. She wasn't trying to get Matthew's attention, but she couldn't help but feel self-conscious under his gaze.

The beauty mark above her left eyebrow seemed to itch, and she resisted the urge to touch it.

Meanwhile, on the other side of the lawn, Zack and Matthew continued their conversation. Zack's muscular frame was drenched in sweat, his swim trunks clinging to his toned abs. He tossed the football casually as he spoke, his deep brown eyes locking with Matthew's.

"So, what's the deal with you and Sammy?" Zack asked, his voice laced with curiosity. "You thinking about swapping partners?"

Matthew caught the ball, his grip firm. "I've been thinking about it," he admitted, his eyes flicking toward Sammy. "She's attractive, but... I don't know. She reminds me of my sister."

Zack raised an eyebrow, a smirk playing on his lips. "Your sister's a four-foot-eleven Mexican woman with big tits and ass?"

Matthew chuckled, throwing the ball hard at Zack's gut. "Hey, now. She's mixed like me, but she's short, same age as Sammy. It's just... weird."

Zack rubbed his stomach, feigning pain. "No offense, but your sister doesn't look like that," he said, pointing toward Sammy. She had turned onto her stomach, her derrière prominently displayed as she chatted with Claire. Matthew's gaze followed Zack's gesture, and despite himself, his cock twitched.

"I mean, she's hot," Matthew conceded, shaking his head. "But I wanted to date someone older than twenty-five. Sammy's great, but... I don't know if she's what I'm looking for."

Zack nodded, his expression understanding. "Fair enough. If you're not feeling it, there's no point in lingering. You should swap tomorrow. No use wasting time."

Matthew sighed, running a hand through his curly hair. "Yeah, maybe you're right. I just don't want to hurt her feelings."

As the day wore on, Sammy found herself unable to shake the conversation she'd overheard. She tried to focus on the laughter and music around her, but her mind kept drifting back to Matthew. She watched him from afar, noticing the way he interacted with the other contestants. There was an ease to him, a charm that drew people in. But with her, it felt different. Distant.

That evening, as the sun dipped below the horizon, painting the sky in hues of orange and pink, Sammy sat alone on one of the poolside loungers. The villa was quieter now, the energy of the day giving way to a more relaxed atmosphere. She traced the rim of her pineapple cocktail with her finger, her thoughts a tangled mess. The ice clinked against the glass, a sharp contrast to the silence in her mind.

Claire approached, a concerned look on her face. "You okay?" she asked, sitting down beside her. Her slim frame and bright smile were a stark contrast to Sammy's curvy, brooding figure.

Sammy sighed, setting her drink aside. The condensation on the glass left a damp ring on the wooden table. "I don't know, Claire. I really like Matthew, but... it's like he's holding back. And now I'm starting to wonder if I'm just not his type. Maybe he's not into curvy girls like me."

Claire placed a hand on her arm, her touch reassuring. "You're amazing, Sammy. Anyone would be lucky to have you. Maybe you just need to have an honest conversation with him. See where his head's at."

Sammy nodded, though doubt still lingered in her eyes. "Maybe you're right. But what if he confirms my worst fears? What if he really does see me as just a friend?"

Claire squeezed her arm gently. "Then you'll know where you stand, and you can move on. You deserve someone who appreciates you for who you are."

As the night deepened, the contestants gathered around the fire pit, the crackling flames casting flickering shadows across their faces. Conversations flowed, laughter echoed, and the tension of the day seemed to melt away—at least for everyone but Sammy. She sat on the edge of the group, her gaze drifting toward Matthew, who was engaged in a lively discussion with Katie. There was an ease to their interaction, a familiarity that made Sammy's chest tighten.

She took a deep breath, steeling herself. If she was going to figure out where she stood with Matthew, she needed to talk to him. Now.

With a determined nod, she stood, her heart pounding in her chest. The cool night air brushed against her skin as she made her way across the patio. Matthew noticed her approach and smiled, his expression warm but guarded.

"Hey," he said, his deep voice sending a shiver down her spine.

"Hey," she replied, her voice steady despite her nerves. "Can we talk?"

Matthew's smile faltered, just for a moment, before he nodded. "Of course. Let's take a walk."

They strolled along the beach, the sand cool beneath their feet, the waves crashing rhythmically in the distance. The moon hung low in the sky, casting a silvery glow over the water. Sammy felt the weight of the moment pressing down on her, but she forced herself to speak.

"Matthew, I... I've been thinking a lot today," she began, her voice soft but firm. "About us. Or... whatever this is."

He glanced at her, his expression unreadable. "What about it?"

She took a deep breath, her heart pounding in her chest. "I feel like we're not really moving forward. I mean, we haven't even kissed yet, and... I don't know. It's just confusing. I'm starting to wonder if we're even on the same page."

Matthew stopped walking, turning to face her. The moonlight illuminated his features, highlighting the freckles scattered across his nose and the scruff on his jaw. He looked at her for a long moment, his gaze intense, before speaking.

"Sammy, I... I like you," he said, his voice low and sincere. "You're beautiful, and funny, and... you remind me of someone I care about. That's why it's been hard for me to... move forward. I don't want to rush into something if it's not right."

Sammy's heart ached at his words. She understood his hesitation, but it didn't make the rejection any less painful. "So... what are you saying? That we should just... stay friends?"

Matthew sighed, running a hand through his hair. "I'm saying I need to figure some things out. Maybe... maybe we should take a step back. See if there's someone else here who's a better fit for both of us."

Sammy felt tears prick at the corners of her eyes, but she forced herself to nod. "Okay," she whispered, her voice breaking. "If that's what you want."

They stood there for a moment longer, the silence between them heavy with unspoken emotions. Then, with a nod, Matthew turned and walked back toward the villa, leaving Sammy alone on the beach.

She sank to the sand, the cool grains seeping through her bikini bottoms as she wrapped her arms around her knees. Tears streamed down her cheeks, and she let them fall, the salt mixing with the bitterness in her mouth. She had come to Love Oasis hoping to find love, but instead, she felt more lost than ever.

As she sat there, the sounds of laughter and music from the villa drifted across the beach, a stark contrast to her own heartbreak. She knew she had to pull herself together, to put on a brave face and pretend everything was okay. But in that moment, all she could do was let herself feel the pain.

The night deepened around her, the stars twinkling above like distant reminders of possibilities yet to come. Sammy took a deep breath, wiping her tears away with the back of her hand. She didn't know what the future held, but she knew one thing for certain: she wasn't going to let this defeat her. Not now. Not ever.

With a determined nod, she stood, brushing the sand from her skin. The cool night air kissed her cheeks as she walked back to the villa, her steps steady despite the turmoil in her heart. She would face tomorrow, whatever it brought. And maybe, just maybe, she would find the love she was searching for—even if it wasn't with Matthew.

Back at the villa, the party was still in full swing, but Sammy felt like an outsider looking in. She grabbed a fresh drink from the bar, the cold glass a welcome distraction. As she sipped her cocktail, she noticed Zack watching her from across the room. His muscular frame was relaxed, but his eyes held a knowing look, as if he could sense her pain.

He approached her, his stride confident yet gentle. "You okay?" he asked, his voice low and concerned.

Sammy forced a smile, though it felt brittle. "Yeah, I'm fine. Just... thinking."

Zack nodded, his expression understanding. "If you ever want to talk, I'm here. No judgment."

She appreciated his kindness, but the last thing she wanted was to burden someone else with her problems. "Thanks, Zack. I might take you up on that."

As the night wore on, Sammy found herself drawn into a game of truth or dare with a group of contestants. The laughter and teasing helped take her mind off Matthew, if only for a little while. But when the game ended, and she was left alone with her thoughts, the pain returned, sharper than before.

She retreated to her shared room with Matthew, the cool tiles of the floor a welcome relief against her bare feet. As she lay in bed next to Matthew, the moonlight streaming through the sheer curtains, she replayed the conversation with Matthew in her mind. His words echoed in her head, and she couldn't shake the feeling of rejection. She thought about talking to him more, but heard him softly snoring beside her and decided against it.

But amidst the pain, a spark of determination ignited within her. She refused to let this define her. She knew her worth, and she wouldn't let one man's hesitation hold her back.

Chapter 7

The night air was thick with anticipation as the group gathered at the Love Oasis villa, the soft glow of string lights casting a warm, golden ambiance over the poolside area. The women, dressed in form-fitting mini dresses that hugged their curves, exuded a sultry confidence, their laughter mingling with the rhythmic beats of the music playing in the background. Sammy, her olive skin radiant under the soft lighting, stood by the bar, her dress accentuating her busty figure and toned legs. She felt a mix of excitement and nervousness as she watched Matthew across the room. He leaned against the wall, his tall, lanky frame relaxed, his curly hair catching the light, and his light brown skin glowing with a subtle warmth. Their earlier conversation replayed in her mind, the unspoken tension between them lingering like a promise waiting to be fulfilled. Tonight was about letting go, about embracing the moment, and she was determined to do just that.

Victoria, her long brunette hair cascading down her back, stood beside Xavier, her enhanced figure turning heads as she laughed at something he whispered. Claire, in a sleek black dress that contrasted beautifully with her beige skin and wavy black hair, was deep in conversation with Zack, whose muscular frame and neatly trimmed goatee exuded a quiet confidence. Yolanda, her curvy figure accentuated by a tight-fitting red dress, was sipping a drink with Will, his sandy blond hair catching the light as he leaned in to say something that made her laugh. Katie, her blonde hair shimmering under the lights, stood apart, her blue eyes scanning the room with a mix of curiosity and detachment.

As Travis lined up shots of vibrant blue liquor, the group gathered around, the clinking of glasses filling the air with a festive sound. "To love, to lust, and to everything in between!" Zack proclaimed, his deep voice cutting through the music. The others cheered, their voices blending in a chorus of agreement. Sammy took her shot, the burn of the alcohol warming her throat, and felt a buzz of excitement as the group moved towards the dance floor.

The music pulsed through the speakers, a mix of sultry R&B and upbeat pop, drawing the couples closer together. Sammy watched as Claire and Zack moved in sync, their bodies swaying to the rhythm, their laughter infectious. Yolanda and Will were locked in a passionate embrace, their movements fluid and sensual, their chemistry undeniable. Even Victoria and Xavier seemed to have found a rhythm, their bodies moving in perfect harmony, their eyes locked on each other as if no one else existed.

Matthew approached Katie, his hand extending towards her, a hopeful smile on his face. But she stepped back, a slight frown creasing her forehead. "I'm good, thanks," she said, her voice cool, her southern accent noticeable. Matthew's smile faltered, a flicker of disappointment crossing his face. Before he could respond, Sammy was there, her hand on his arm, her vibrant smile reassuring. "Come on, Matthew," she said, her voice soft but insistent. "Let's dance."

He hesitated for a moment, his eyes flicking between Katie and Sammy, before allowing himself to be led onto the dance floor. The music enveloped them, and Sammy moved closer, her body swaying gently against his. She could feel his tension, the stiffness in his movements, and she smiled, her hand resting lightly on his chest. "Just let go," she whispered, her breath warm against his ear. "It's just us here."

Slowly, Matthew relaxed, his arms wrapping around her waist, his hands resting gently on the small of her back. They moved together, their bodies in sync, the music guiding them. Sammy felt a spark, a connection, as their eyes met, and she knew in that moment that this was what she'd been waiting for. The air around them seemed to hum with possibility, the scent of tropical flowers and the faint chlorine from the pool blending into a heady mix.

As the song ended, the group cheered, their voices filled with laughter and excitement. "Spin the bottle!" Travis shouted, his voice cutting through the music. The others agreed, their enthusiasm palpable as they formed a circle on the plush outdoor rugs, the bottle placed in the center. The game was a villa tradition, a way to break the ice and explore the unspoken tensions that simmered beneath the surface.

Matthew spun the bottle first, his heart racing as it slowed, coming to a stop pointing at Katie. He hesitated, his mind flashing back to their earlier conversation, the unspoken distance between them. But the group was already cheering, egging him on. He took a deep breath and leaned in, his lips brushing against her cheek. The room erupted in boos, and Katie rolled her eyes, her expression a mix of annoyance and detachment. "I'm committed to the man I'm with," she said, her voice firm, her blue eyes meeting Matthew's with a challenge.

Zack spun next, the bottle landing on Claire. The room fell silent as they leaned in, their lips meeting in a kiss that seemed to last an eternity. Claire's eyes fluttered closed, her breath catching as the kiss deepened, her hands resting lightly on Zack's broad shoulders. When they finally parted, she was breathless, a dazed smile on her face, her cheeks flushed. "Wow," she whispered, her voice barely audible.

Sammy's turn came next, her heart pounding as she spun the bottle. It landed on Matthew, and she felt a rush of anticipation. She leaned in, her lips brushing against his, the kiss starting soft and tentative before deepening. Matthew's arms wrapped around her, his hands tangling in her long dark hair, as the kiss became more passionate. Sammy's mind went blank, the world around her fading away as she lost herself in the moment. The taste of his lips, the warmth of his skin, the scent of his cologne—it all blended into a sensory overload that left her breathless.

When they finally parted, the room was silent, the only sound the soft music playing in the background. Matthew's eyes met Sammy's, his expression unreadable, and she felt a flutter in her chest, a mix of excitement and uncertainty. The air between them crackled with unspoken tension, the moment stretching into an eternity before the group erupted into cheers and whistles, breaking the spell.

The game continued, the bottle spinning, landing on different couples, each kiss more intense than the last. Sammy watched as Claire and Zack shared another passionate moment, their connection undeniable. She saw the way Yolanda and Will moved together, their chemistry electric, their kisses filled with a raw intensity. Even Victoria and Xavier seemed to have found a rhythm, their kisses deep and lingering, their bodies pressed close.

But it was Matthew's kiss that stayed with her, the memory of his lips on hers, the feel of his hands on her skin. She caught his eye across the room, and he looked away, a flush creeping up his neck, his scruffy beard catching the light. Sammy smiled, a secret smile, knowing that something had shifted between them, something undeniable and exciting.

As the night wore on, the group settled into a comfortable silence, the game forgotten as they lounged by the pool, the stars twinkling above. Sammy lay on a lounge chair, her head resting on her arms, her eyes on Matthew as he sat on the edge of the pool, his feet dangling in the water. He seemed lost in thought, his eyes distant, the moonlight casting a silver glow over his freckled skin. She wondered what he was thinking, if he felt the same connection she did.

The others chatted softly, their voices blending into a soothing hum, but Sammy's mind was elsewhere, her thoughts drifting to the future, to the possibilities that lay ahead. She knew that tomorrow they would have to make a decision, to stay or switch partners, and she felt a surge of anxiety at the thought. But as she looked at Matthew, at the way his curly hair caught the light, at the way his lips curved into a smile as he laughed at something Zack said, she knew that she wanted to explore this, to see where it could go.

Matthew stood, stretching his long limbs, and Sammy's heart skipped a beat as he approached her. "Hey," he said, his voice soft, his deep southern accent wrapping around her like a warm blanket. "Can I talk to you?"

She sat up, her heart racing, and nodded, following him as he led her to a quiet corner of the patio. The night air was cool against her skin, the scent of tropical flowers filling her senses as they sat down, their knees touching. The soft glow of the string lights cast a romantic ambiance, the world around them fading into the background.

"I wanted to apologize," Matthew began, his voice serious, his eyes searching hers. "For earlier, for not being more... present. I've been a jerk, and I'm sorry."

Sammy smiled, a soft, understanding smile. "It's okay," she said, her voice gentle. "We all have our moments. But I appreciate you saying that."

He nodded, his eyes intense, his freckles standing out in the dim light. "I've been thinking a lot about us, about what we have. And I realize now that I've been holding back, afraid to fully commit. But after tonight, after that kiss..." He trailed off, his cheeks flushing, his scruffy beard twitching as he spoke. "I want to give this a fair shot. I want to be all in, with you."

Sammy's heart swelled, a warmth spreading through her chest. "I want that too," she said, her voice steady, her eyes meeting his. "I want to explore this, to see where it can go. But we have to be honest with each other, no more holding back."

Matthew nodded, his eyes locked on hers, his expression resolute. "No more holding back," he agreed. "I'm ready to take a leap of faith, if you are."

She smiled, reaching out to take his hand. "I'm ready," she said, her voice filled with conviction. "Let's do this together."

As their fingers intertwined, a spark passed between them, a silent promise of what was to come. The night air seemed to shimmer around them, the stars twinkling in approval, as they sat there, hand in hand, the world around them fading away. In that moment, Sammy knew that she was falling, falling hard and fast for Matthew, and she couldn't wait to see where this journey would take them.

As they rejoined the group, the laughter and music welcoming them back, Sammy felt a sense of peace, a sense of belonging. She glanced at Matthew, their hands still intertwined, and smiled, knowing that this was just the beginning, the start of something beautiful and unpredictable.

The night deepened, the stars shining brighter, as the group continued to laugh and chat, their voices blending into a harmonious melody. Sammy and Matthew sat together, their shoulders touching, their hands clasped, a silent understanding passing between them. The others seemed to sense the shift, their smiles warm and knowing as they teased the couple lightly.

As the first light of dawn began to creep over the horizon, casting a soft pink glow over the villa, Sammy knew that this was a night she would never forget, a night that would change everything. And as she looked at Matthew, his eyes meeting hers in a silent promise, she knew that she was exactly where she was meant to be. The future was uncertain, but with him by her side, she was ready to face whatever came their way.

Matthew stood, offering his hand to Sammy. "Let's go," he said, his voice low, his eyes filled with determination. She took his hand, feeling a surge of excitement as they walked towards their room, the others waving them off with smiles and knowing glances. As they entered the room, the cameras capturing their every move, Sammy turned to Matthew, her heart racing.

"Are you sure about this?" she asked, her voice soft, her eyes searching his.

He pulled her close, his hands resting on her hips, his eyes intense. "I've never been more sure of anything in my life," he whispered, his lips brushing against hers.

Sammy smiled, a secret smile, as she wrapped her arms around his neck. "Then let's make this real," she said, her voice filled with conviction.

Their kiss deepened, their bodies pressing together, the world around them fading away. Sammy giggled, covering their bodies with a blanket to block the cameras, her laughter infectious as Matthew joined in. Their kiss deepened further, their passion igniting as they explored each other, their touches tender yet urgent. In that moment, Matthew realized that although he didn't know how his future was going to be in the villa, he did know one thing: he was catching feelings for Sammy, and he was ready to see where this journey would take them.

Chapter 8

The morning sun bathed the Love Oasis villa in a warm, golden light, its rays filtering through the palm trees and casting dappled shadows across the pool's shimmering surface. The air was alive with the scent of blooming hibiscus and the faint tang of saltwater, a reminder of the ocean just beyond the villa's walls. The contestants emerged from their rooms one by one, their footsteps echoing on the stone pathways as they made their way to the workout area. The previous night's spin-the-bottle game had left an electric charge in the air, and everyone was buzzing with excitement and curiosity about what the day would bring.

Matthew was the first to arrive at the workout space, his curly hair still damp from a quick shower. He leaned against the weight bench, a sly grin spreading across his face as the others began to trickle in. His light brown skin glistened with a sheen of sweat, and his scruffy beard gave him a rugged charm that seemed to draw everyone's attention. "Y'all won't believe what happened last night," he drawled, his deep southern accent wrapping around the words like a warm blanket. "Sammy and I, we really connected. I mean, really connected. It's like we're on the same wavelength, you know?"

Zack, towering over the bench press with his muscular frame and neatly trimmed goatee, let out a low whistle. His ebony skin glistened under the fluorescent lights, and his multiple tattoos seemed to dance across his arms and chest. "No way, man. You and Sammy? That's... unexpected. But hey, if it's real, I'm all for it."

Travis, his tanned arms crossed over his chest, smirked. His slicked-back black hair and gold chain necklace gave him a sleek, confident air. "Yeah, man, you finally found someone who can keep up with your charm. Good for you."

Matthew's grin widened, his freckles standing out against his skin like tiny constellations. "I'm telling you, it's different with her. She's not like the others. There's something about her that just... clicks, you know? It's like we're speaking the same language without even trying."

Will, his sandy blond hair still tousled from sleep, chimed in. "Well, if you're serious about this, you better make it official. Raven's gonna be asking us to swap or stay soon. You gotta decide if you're all in or not."

Matthew's expression turned thoughtful, his gaze drifting toward the pool area where Sammy was laughing with Yolanda. Sammy's long dark hair cascaded over her shoulders, and her vibrant smile lit up the morning like a beacon. "I am, man. I'm all in. I've never felt this way before. It's like... I can be myself around her, you know? No pretenses, no games. Just... us."

Zack's brow furrowed, his usually confident demeanor faltering for a moment. "What about you, man? You gonna swap or stay with Claire?" The question hung in the air like a challenge, and Zack's eyes flicked toward the pool, where Claire was sitting on a lounge chair, her long black hair cascading over her shoulders as she chatted animatedly with Yolanda. Claire's bright smile and slim figure were a stark contrast to Sammy's curvy, bold presence, and Zack's hesitation was palpable.

"I don't know, man," he admitted, his voice low. "Claire's... she's amazing. We connected over anime and all, but there's something holding me back. I mean, she's smart, funny, and we have a lot in common, but it's like there's a wall between us. I can't quite put my finger on it."

Matthew clapped a hand on Zack's shoulder, his expression sympathetic. "Take your time, brother. These decisions ain't easy. But whatever you choose, we got your back."

The conversation shifted as the rest of the group joined in, each sharing their thoughts on the night before and the impending decision. Victoria, her long brunette hair cascading down her back, spoke up, her voice laced with a hint of Italian accent. "Love is complicated, no? You have to follow your heart, but sometimes your heart doesn't know what it wants."

Xavier, his dark skin adorned with intricate tattoos, nodded in agreement. "It's about trust, too. You gotta trust your instincts, but also be willing to take a leap of faith."

Katie, her blonde hair shimmering in the morning light, added, "And don't forget to communicate. If you're not on the same page, it's only gonna lead to heartbreak."

As the discussion deepened, the workout area became a melting pot of emotions and advice, each contestant bringing their own perspective to the table. The morning sun climbed higher in the sky, casting longer shadows across the villa, and the air grew warmer, heavy with the weight of their collective thoughts.

Later that night, the villa was transformed into a dazzling spectacle. The pool area was illuminated by strings of twinkling fairy lights and the soft glow of lanterns, their flickering flames casting a romantic ambiance. The contestants, dressed in their most alluring outfits, gathered on the platforms, their hearts pounding with anticipation. Raven, resplendent in a vibrant sundress that showcased her cleavage and long legs, took center stage. Her platinum blonde hair cascaded in loose waves down her back, and her piercing blue eyes seemed to see right through each of them.

"Alright, my loves," she purred, her British accent lending a sultry edge to her words. "It's time to make some decisions. You've had a chance to get to know each other, to explore the connections you've formed. Now, it's time to decide: do you want to swap or stay?"

The air crackled with electricity as Raven began with Matthew and Sammy, her gaze intense and unwavering. "Matthew, Sammy," she intoned, her voice carrying across the silent crowd. "Do you want to stay or swap?"

Matthew stepped forward, his gaze locked on Sammy's, his expression unwavering. "I want to stay," he declared, his voice steady and filled with conviction. "Sammy's not just a pretty face, she's got a heart of gold. She's funny, she's smart, and she's got this energy about her that's just... infectious. I want to get to know her, to really explore this connection we have. It's like she's this puzzle I can't wait to solve, and every piece I uncover makes me want her more."

Sammy's eyes shone with unshed tears as she turned to Raven, her voice trembling with emotion. "I want to stay too. Matthew's been honest with me from the start, and that's something I've been searching for. He's got this way of making me feel seen, you know? Like I'm not just another face in the crowd. He listens to me, really listens, and it's like he understands me on a level no one else ever has. I want to see where this goes, to see if this connection we have can grow into something even more amazing."

A collective sigh of relief rippled through the group as Raven nodded, her expression approving. "Very well. You may stay together."

The night continued with each couple facing their moment of truth. Zack, after a moment of hesitation, stepped forward, his voice steady as he declared his decision. "I want to stay with Claire," he said, his gaze locked on her. "There's something about her that draws me in, something I can't quite explain. Maybe it's the way she lights up when she talks about anime, or how she can make me laugh even when I'm feeling down. I want to figure it out, to see where this road takes us. I'm not ready to give up on us just yet."

Claire's eyes widened, a soft smile playing on her lips as she turned to Raven. "I want to stay too. Zack's got this... depth to him, you know? He's not just a pretty face. There's more to him than meets the eye, and I want to uncover those layers. I want to know what makes him tick, what his dreams are, and what scares him. I think there's something special between us, something worth fighting for."

One by one, the contestants made their decisions, each moment filled with tension and emotion. Xavier and Victoria chose to stay together, their connection undeniable. Yolanda and Will decided to swap, both acknowledging that while they enjoyed each other's company, their relationship lacked the spark they were seeking. Travis and Katie, after a heartfelt conversation, chose to swap too. With that Will and Katie were a couple and Travis and Yolanda were an item now, although it didn't seem like Travis was particularly happy about being with Yolanda.

As the final decisions were made, Raven's expression turned solemn, her voice taking on a note of finality. "Remember, my loves, the power is in your hands. You've chosen your paths, now it's up to you to make the most of them. In three days, America will decide who they want to see stay together. Until then, enjoy the ride, cherish these moments, and never forget why you came here in the first place."

With that, the group erupted into cheers and applause, the tension of the night giving way to a sense of celebration and camaraderie. The villa came alive with music and laughter, the contestants dancing under the stars, their hearts light with anticipation. Sammy and Matthew, their arms wrapped around each other, shared a tender kiss, their lips brushing softly as the world around them faded away.

"I'm so glad we get to explore this," Matthew murmured, his lips brushing against Sammy's ear, sending shivers down her spine. "You're amazing, you know that? You've got this fire inside you, this passion that's contagious. I can't wait to see where this journey takes us."

Sammy laughed, her eyes sparkling with mischief. "I know. But seriously, Matthew, I'm happy too. This feels... right, you know? Like we're meant to be on this journey together. It's like the universe conspired to bring us together, and I'm just gonna go with it and see where it leads."

As the night deepened, the group retired to their rooms, their minds racing with thoughts of the future. Sammy and Matthew, curled up together in bed, their bodies entwined, felt a sense of peace wash over them. The uncertainty of the past few days melted away in the warmth of their embrace, replaced by a quiet confidence in their decision.

"I'm happy we get to do this together," Matthew whispered, his fingers tracing patterns on Sammy's arm, his touch gentle and soothing. "You're something special, Sammy Rodriguez. Don't ever forget that. You've got this light inside you, this spark that makes everything brighter. I feel lucky to be the one who gets to see it every day."

Sammy smiled, her eyes drifting closed as she snuggled closer to Matthew, the sound of his heartbeat lulling her into a sense of security and belonging. "I won't," she murmured. "And neither should you, Matthew Brown. You're pretty special too. You've got this way of making me feel like I'm the only person in the room, like I'm the most important thing in your world. That's a pretty amazing gift, and I'm grateful to have you in my life."

As they drifted off to sleep, the villa fell silent, the only sound the gentle lapping of the pool's water against the edge, a soothing melody that seemed to whisper secrets of love, connection, and the magic that lay just beyond the horizon. The journey was far from over, but for now, in this moment, everything felt right, everything felt possible. The future stretched out before them like an unwritten book, full of promise and potential, and they were ready to turn the page together.

Chapter 9

The villa buzzed with life, the late afternoon sun casting long shadows across the marble floors as the boys gathered in the courtyard, their laughter echoing off the whitewashed walls. Matthew, his tall, lanky frame leaning casually against the fountain's edge, grinned as he held up a can of whipped cream. "Alright, fellas, let's break up this tension. Those girls have been cooped up all day—time to give 'em something to remember." His deep southern drawl carried a mischievous edge, his curly hair catching the sunlight as he tossed the can to one of the guys.

Sammy, meanwhile, was lounging by the pool with the other girls, her olive skin glowing under the sun. Her tiny bikini top and string thong bottoms accentuated her curvy figure, and her long dark hair cascaded in loose waves down her back. She laughed as she sipped a fruity drink, her vibrant smile lighting up the area. Her distinctive beauty mark above her left eyebrow seemed to sparkle with her every expression. "You know, I think the boys are up to something," she teased, her eyes scanning the courtyard. "They've been awfully quiet."

The boys, armed with whipped cream cans and pies, crept toward the pool area, their whispers and giggles betraying their plan. Matthew, leading the charge, had a whipped cream pie clutched in his hands, his eyes locked on Sammy. "Here goes nothing," he muttered, his heart racing with a mix of excitement and nervousness.

Sammy, sensing something amiss, turned just as Matthew lunged forward, the pie smashing into her face with a splat. Whipped cream covered her cheeks, nose, and lips, but instead of anger, she burst into laughter. "Matthew Brown, you are so dead!" she shrieked, her voice filled with playful indignation.

"Oh, you're all dirty now," Matthew teased, his eyes crinkling at the corners as he laughed. "Guess I'll have to clean you up."

Sammy raised an eyebrow, her laughter fading into a mischievous smile. "Oh yeah? And how do you plan on doing that?"

Matthew's grin widened, and without hesitation, he leaned in, his fingers gently cupping her face as he licked the whipped cream from her cheeks. The courtyard erupted into cheers and whistles from the other contestants, but Sammy's attention was solely on Matthew. His touch was warm, his breath tickling her skin, and for a moment, the world around them seemed to fade away.

"You missed a spot," Sammy said, her voice soft but laced with challenge, as she pointed to her breasts, where a dollop of whipped cream clung to her bikini top.

Matthew's eyes followed her finger, and his grin turned into a full-blown laugh. "How could I forget?" he said, his voice low and playful. With deliberate slowness, he leaned down, his lips brushing against her skin as he licked the cream away. The air crackled with tension, and Sammy's breath hitched, her heart pounding in her chest.

When he pulled back, Matthew's expression softened, his eyes searching hers. "You know, Sammy, I've been thinking. I'd really like to take you on a proper date. Just the two of us. No pranks, no one else. Just me, cooking for you."

Sammy's smile returned, warm and genuine. "A date, huh? And what makes you think I'd say yes?"

"Because," Matthew said, his voice steady, "I'm a damn good cook, and I've got a feeling you're worth the effort."

Sammy laughed, a light, infectious sound that made Matthew's heart skip a beat. "Alright, Matthew Brown. You've got yourself a date. But if your cooking's as bad as your pranks, I'm holding you responsible."

A few hours later, after the villa was a cleaned of their mess of whipped cream, pie crusts, Matthew, now cleaned up and dressed in a simple white shirt and jeans, stood in the kitchen, his sleeves rolled preparing dinner. The scent of frying chicken filled the air, mingling with the sweet aroma of candied yams and the earthy smell of greens simmering on the stove.

Sammy entered the kitchen, her sundress a stunning shade of coral that complemented her olive skin perfectly. The low-cut neckline accentuated her busty figure, and her hair was styled in loose waves that framed her face. Matthew's breath caught in his throat as he turned to face her, his hands pausing mid-action. "Wow," he murmured, his voice thick with admiration. "You look... incredible."

Sammy smiled, her cheeks flushing slightly as she twirled in a small circle. "Thanks. Thought I'd dress up for our date. You know, since it's official and all."

Matthew chuckled, shaking his head as he gestured to the table he'd set with care. "Food's almost ready. Hope you're hungry."

As they sat down to eat, the table was a feast for the eyes. The fried chicken was golden and crispy, the candied yams glistened with a sticky sweetness, and the greens were seasoned to perfection. Sammy picked up a piece of chicken, her eyes widening in delight as she took her first bite. "Mmm, this is amazing!" she exclaimed, her voice muffled around the food. "Your mama would be proud."

Matthew beamed, his pride evident. "Told you I could handle a skillet. This is one of my favorites from back home. Reminds me of Sunday dinners with the family."

Sammy's expression softened as she listened to him talk about his childhood in Snow Hill, about the farm and the close-knit community. "It sounds so different from Houston," she remarked, her voice tinged with nostalgia. "Although I grew up in the city, my mom always made sure we had big family meals. She taught me a lot of Mexican dishes—that's actually my favorite cuisine."

Matthew's eyes lit up. "Mexican? Now that's a challenge I'd love to take on. If you let me cook for you again, I'll let you cook for me. Deal?"

Sammy laughed, her eyes sparkling with mischief. "Deal. I can't wait for you to taste my Mexican."

Matthew raised an eyebrow, a playful smirk tugging at his lips. "Was that supposed to be sexual? Because the way you said 'taste my Mexican' is making me think otherwise."

Sammy gasped dramatically, slapping his hand lightly. "Get your mind out of the gutter, Matthew Brown! However since your mind is there, you can taste me for dessert, but you gotta eat all your veggies first."

Matthew laughed, a deep, hearty sound that filled the kitchen. "I'd eat a whole field of veggies for your dessert, Sammy Rodriguez."

She playfully slapped his shoulder, her laughter mingling with his. "Oh, stop it! You're making me blush."

As they ate, the conversation flowed easily, their banter light and filled with laughter. But beneath the surface, there was a lingering sexual tension, a spark that neither could ignore. The way Matthew's eyes lingered on her when he thought she wasn't looking, the way Sammy's hand brushed his under the table—it was all building toward something more.

When the plates were empty and the dishes cleared, Matthew leaned back in his chair, his eyes meeting Sammy's across the table. "So, about that dessert..." he said, his voice low and teasing.

Sammy's smile was slow and deliberate as she stood, her sundress swaying gently with her movements. "I think you've earned it. But first..." She walked over to the stereo and turned on a soft, sultry song, the rhythm filling the room. "Dance with me."

Matthew hesitated for only a moment before standing, his hand extending toward her. "I'm not much of a dancer, but for you, I'll give it a shot."

As they moved closer, their bodies swaying to the music, the air between them crackled with unspoken desire. Matthew's hand rested at the small of her back, his touch warm and firm, while Sammy's hand rested on his shoulder, her fingers brushing against his skin. Their eyes locked, and for a moment, the world around them ceased to exist.

"You know," Sammy whispered, her breath warm against his ear, "I think you're ready for that dessert now."

Matthew's heart raced, his pulse pounding in his ears. "I think you're right," he murmured, his voice hoarse with want.

But just as he leaned in, the sound of laughter and voices from the living room interrupted their moment. Sammy's eyes flickered toward the door, a fleeting moment of hesitation crossing her face. "We should... we should probably join the others," she said, her voice unsteady.

Matthew nodded, his hand brushing her cheek, his touch gentle. "Yeah," he agreed, his voice thick with regret. "But this... this isn't over, Sammy. Not by a long shot."

She smiled, her eyes sparkling with a promise he couldn't quite decipher. "I'll be counting on it, Matthew Brown."

As they left the kitchen, the warmth of their connection lingering between them, the sounds of the villa grew louder, the laughter and chatter of their fellow contestants a stark contrast to the intimate moment they'd just shared. The night was young, and the possibilities seemed endless.

In the midst of the chaos and the cameras, Matthew and Sammy had found a connection, a spark that threatened to ignite into something more. As they rejoined the group, their hands brushing ever so slightly, they both knew that their romance was beginning to bloom. However the question remained: would they have the courage to explore the depths of their feelings, or would the pressures of the villa and their own fears hold them back?

Only time would tell.

Chapter 10

The villa was alive with anticipation, the air crackling with excitement as the contestants gathered around the shimmering pool. The sun hung high in the Hawaiian sky, casting a golden glow over the lush tropical gardens and the vibrant crowd. The scent of coconut sunscreen mingled with the sweet fragrance of plumeria flowers, creating an intoxicating aroma that seemed to heighten the sense of occasion. Laughter and chatter filled the space, a symphony of voices that rose and fell like the waves lapping at the nearby shore. It was clear that something extraordinary was about to unfold, and the contestants were buzzing with curiosity and nervous energy.

Raven Castaway, the villa's charismatic host, stood on a small stage adorned with colorful banners and tropical flowers. Her presence was magnetic, her confidence commanding the attention of everyone present. Dressed in a flowing silk robe that shimmered in the sunlight, she raised her hands, and the crowd fell silent. "Welcome, lovebirds, to our next adventure!" she announced, her voice rich and melodic, carrying effortlessly across the villa. "Today, we're diving into uncharted territory—a challenge that will test not only your creativity but also the depth of your connection with your partners. It's time for Making Art!"

A murmur of excitement rippled through the crowd. Sammy Rodriguez, her olive skin radiant in the sunlight, felt a flutter of anticipation in her chest. She had always been drawn to creative expression, whether it was through her bold fashion choices or her playful interactions with others. The idea of combining art with physical intimacy intrigued her, and she couldn't help but wonder what the challenge would entail. Beside her, Matthew Brown adjusted his swim trunks, his tall, lanky frame exuding a quiet confidence. He wasn't one for grand gestures or flashy displays, but there was a determination in his eyes that suggested he was ready to make this challenge unforgettable for both himself and Sammy.

"Here's how it works," Raven continued, her eyes sparkling with mischief. She paused for dramatic effect, her gaze sweeping over the crowd before she revealed the details. "Each of you will be paired up, and you'll be given a canvas, paint, and brushes. But here's the twist—you'll also be covered in paint yourselves. And while you're creating your masterpiece, you'll need to create a connection. You'll pick a partner to make out with, grinding your bodies together as you paint. The more passionate, the more creative, the better your chances of winning a special date."

The contestants erupted into cheers and whispers, the atmosphere electric with anticipation. Sammy's heart raced as she imagined what it would be like to be covered in paint, her body pressed against Matthew's. She glanced at him, their eyes meeting for a fleeting moment, and saw a hint of a smile playing on his lips. He gave her a subtle nod, as if to say, Let's make this unforgettable. The unspoken agreement between them sent a thrill through her, and she felt a surge of excitement for what was to come.

The contestants were handed their costumes—sexy, revealing artist outfits that left little to the imagination. Sammy slipped into hers, the fabric hugging her curves in all the right places. The tiny bikini top accentuated her busty figure, while the string thong bottoms showcased her toned physique. Her long dark hair, styled in loose waves, cascaded over her shoulders, and the beauty mark above her left eyebrow added a touch of distinctive charm. Matthew, shirtless and wearing only his swim trunks, looked every bit the rugged island adventurer. His light brown skin glistened in the sunlight, his curly shaggy hair and scruffy beard giving him a carefree yet alluring appearance. Together, they were a striking pair, their contrasting styles complementing each other perfectly.

As the challenge began, the villa transformed into a kaleidoscope of color and chaos. Paint flew through the air, splattering onto canvases, bodies, and the surrounding area. The contestants moved with abandon, their laughter and shouts mingling with the upbeat music playing in the background. Sammy and Matthew stood before their canvas, their eyes locked, an unspoken understanding passing between them. Without a word, they moved closer, the distance between them disappearing as Matthew's hands found Sammy's waist, pulling her against him. She wrapped her arms around his neck, her fingers tangling in his curly hair, and their lips met in a kiss that was both tender and fierce.

The paint smeared between them as they pressed their bodies together, the coolness of it contrasting with the heat of their passion. Sammy could feel Matthew's heartbeat against her chest, his breath warm on her skin. She moved her hips against his, feeling the hardness of his body through the thin fabric of his trunks. The crowd around them cheered, their voices blending with the music, but Sammy and Matthew were lost in their own world. It was as if they were the only two people in the villa, their connection intensifying with every passing moment.

Sammy twerked against Matthew, her movements deliberate and sensual, her curves accentuated by the paint that clung to her skin. The crowd erupted into applause, their cheers fueling the intensity of the moment. Matthew's hands tightened on her hips, holding her close as their kisses deepened. Their bodies moved in rhythm, the paint becoming a part of their intimate dance. It was clear to everyone watching that the sexual tension between them was off the charts, their chemistry undeniable.

As they worked on the canvas, their movements became more synchronized, their bodies creating a living, breathing work of art. Sammy's laughter mingled with Matthew's soft murmurs, their connection deepening with every stroke of the brush. At one point, Matthew whispered into her ear, his deep southern accent sending shivers down her spine. "I think we're supposed to be painting the canvas, not each other," he teased, his breath tickling her earlobe.

Sammy pulled back slightly, her eyes sparkling with amusement. "Who says we can't do both?" she replied, her voice playful. She grabbed a handful of paint and smeared it across his chest, her fingers tracing patterns on his skin. Matthew laughed, his eyes crinkling at the corners, and retaliated by painting a streak down her arm. What followed was a playful paint fight, their laughter echoing across the villa as they splattered each other with vibrant colors.

The challenge continued, but Sammy and Matthew were in their own world, their focus entirely on each other. They returned to the canvas, their bodies still pressed together, their movements fluid and passionate. The paint became an extension of their emotions, each stroke reflecting the intensity of their connection. The canvas transformed into a chaotic yet beautiful masterpiece, a testament to their chemistry and creativity.

When the challenge finally came to an end, Sammy and Matthew stood back, their bodies still pressed together, breathless and covered in paint. The villa fell silent for a moment as everyone took in the scene before them. Matthew looked down at the canvas, now a vibrant explosion of colors, and chuckled. "I think I need a moment," he said, his voice laced with amusement. "If I stand up right now, I might poke someone's eye out."

The crowd burst into laughter, and Sammy fanned herself, her cheeks flushed with a mixture of excitement and embarrassment. "That was really hot," she admitted, her voice barely above a whisper. Matthew adjusted his trunks, a slight blush creeping up his neck, and grinned. "Yeah, well, I guess we know who's winning this challenge."

The judges deliberated briefly, their eyes scanning the various canvases and the contestants still catching their breath. Finally, Raven stepped forward, her expression one of pure delight. "And the couple who truly embodied passion, creativity, and connection is... Matthew and Sammy!" she declared, her voice filled with enthusiasm.

The villa erupted into cheers as Sammy and Matthew hugged, their painted bodies still pressed together. The applause was deafening, and Sammy felt a surge of pride and joy. She looked up at Matthew, her eyes shining, and he smiled down at her, his expression soft and full of admiration.

Later that day, the two of them were rewarded with a special date—a snorkeling adventure away from the villa. They arrived at a secluded beach, the turquoise waters inviting and serene. The sand was soft and warm beneath their feet, and the sound of the waves crashing against the shore created a soothing backdrop. As they slipped into the water, the world around them seemed to fade away, leaving only the two of them and the breathtaking underwater world.

The coral reefs were a sight to behold, their vibrant colors and intricate shapes creating a mesmerizing landscape. Tropical fish darted around them in a kaleidoscope of hues, their movements graceful and hypnotic. Sammy swam close to Matthew, her hand brushing against his as they explored the reef. "This is amazing," she whispered, her voice muffled by the snorkel. Matthew nodded, his eyes meeting hers through their masks. "It really is," he agreed, his voice soft but steady.

They swam together, their movements synchronized as if they were dancing underwater. Sammy felt a sense of peace and connection with Matthew that she had never experienced before. The villa and its challenges felt like a distant memory, and in that moment, it was just the two of them, lost in the beauty of the ocean.

After their snorkeling adventure, they sat on the beach, a soft blanket spread out beneath them. A chilled bottle of champagne and a platter of tropical fruit awaited them, the perfect end to their perfect day. Sammy leaned against Matthew, her head resting on his shoulder, as they sipped their champagne and enjoyed the fruit. The sweetness of the pineapple and mango complemented the crispness of the champagne, and Sammy felt a sense of contentment wash over her.

"Today was... incredible," Sammy said, her voice filled with gratitude. She looked up at Matthew, her eyes searching his, and saw the same sentiment reflected in his gaze. Matthew smiled, his hand finding hers and giving it a gentle squeeze. "I'm glad you enjoyed it," he replied, his tone sincere. "I've been wanting to tell you something, Sammy. I'm falling for you. Hard."

Sammy's heart skipped a beat, her breath catching in her throat. She had felt the same way, but hearing Matthew say it aloud made it real. "I feel the same way, Matthew," she confessed, her voice barely above a whisper. Their eyes locked, and the world around them seemed to disappear. Their lips met in a kiss that was both tender and passionate, the sunset painting the sky in hues of orange and pink behind them.

As they sat there, wrapped in each other's arms, the villa and its challenges felt like a distant memory. In that moment, it was just the two of them, their connection deepening with every passing second. The future was uncertain, but one thing was clear—Sammy and Matthew were falling in love, and nothing could stop them.

The sun dipped below the horizon, casting a golden glow over the beach. Sammy and Matthew sat in silence, their hands intertwined, the sound of the waves lulling them into a peaceful tranquility. The villa would continue its drama, its challenges, and its surprises, but for now, they had found their own little piece of paradise.

As they stood to leave, Matthew turned to Sammy, his eyes filled with a warmth she had never seen before. "This isn't the end, Sammy," he said, his voice steady and full of promise. "It's just the beginning."

Sammy smiled, her heart full. "I know," she replied, her voice soft but sure. "And I can't wait to see what's next."

Chapter 11

The villa was alive with anticipation, the air crackling with the energy of the first elimination night. The grand hall, usually a place of laughter and casual flirtation, now buzzed with a different kind of tension. The women, dressed in their most seductive club outfits, exuded a mix of confidence and nervousness. Sammy, in a form-fitting black dress that hugged her curves, stood near the bar, her long dark hair cascading over her shoulders. Her vibrant smile, usually so infectious, was subdued, her beauty mark above her left eyebrow a subtle reminder of her uniqueness. Claire, in a sleek red number that accentuated her slim figure, approached her, her brown eyes filled with concern.

"You okay?" Claire asked, her voice soft, her Korean-American features softened by worry. She placed a hand on Sammy's arm, a gesture of solidarity.

Sammy sighed, her olive skin seeming to pale under the stress. "I don't know, Claire. I just... I really like Matthew. A lot. And now, this elimination... it feels like everything's on the line." She glanced across the room, where Matthew stood with Zack near the workout space. His tall, lanky frame was tense, his light brown skin glistening under the villa's lights. His curly hair, usually so carefree, seemed to weigh heavily on his head.

Claire followed her gaze, her expression sympathetic. "I get it. Zack and I are in the same boat. We've been hitting it off, and the thought of it ending so soon... it sucks." She paused, her bright smile returning briefly. "But you and Matthew, you guys have something special. America has to see that, right?"

Sammy's eyes welled up, and she quickly blinked away the tears. "I hope so. But what if they don't? What if this is it?" She took a shaky breath, her hands twisting together. "I can't bear the thought of losing him before we even really started."

Claire pulled her into a tight hug, the scent of her coconut-scented perfume comforting. "You're not going to lose him. Not tonight. Not ever. You're Sammy Rodriguez, remember? You're bold, you're fearless, and you've got a heart as big as this island. Whatever happens, you'll handle it."

Across the room, Matthew leaned against the marble countertop of the bar, his scruffy beard scratching his hand as he rubbed his face. Zack, his muscular frame towering beside him, clapped a hand on his shoulder. "You alright, man?" Zack's deep voice was laced with genuine concern, his ebony skin gleaming under the villa's lights.

Matthew sighed, his southern accent thick with emotion. "I don't know, Zack. Sammy and I... it's like we just started to figure things out. And now, this elimination. It feels like the universe is playing a cruel joke on us."

Zack nodded, his neatly trimmed goatee bobbing. "I hear you. Claire and I are in the same spot. We're still exploring this thing between us, and the thought of it being cut short... it's a punch in the gut." He paused, his brown eyes locking with Matthew's. "But you know what? Sometimes, these things work out in ways we don't expect. Maybe this is just a test."

Matthew managed a small smile, his freckles standing out on his worried face. "A test, huh? Well, I guess we'll see how we fare."

Before Zack could respond, the sound of Raven's heels clicking against the marble floor echoed through the hall. The conversation halted as all eyes turned toward her. Raven Castaway, the host of the show, stood tall and elegant in a vibrant yellow sundress that showcased her long legs and cleavage. Her platinum blonde hair fell in loose waves down her back, and her piercing blue eyes scanned the room with a mix of authority and empathy.

"Alright, everyone, gather around," Raven announced, her British accent crisp and commanding. "It's time for the elimination results. I'll be calling out the top three voted teams, in no particular order, and then the bottom two."

The room fell silent, the only sound the soft hum of the air conditioning and the distant crash of waves against the shore. The contestants, their hearts pounding, formed a semicircle around Raven. Victoria Chance, her bronzed skin glowing in a tight silver dress, stood beside Xavier Cross, his dark, tattooed arms crossed over his broad chest. Yolanda Smith, her curvy figure accentuated by a low-cut red gown, leaned into Travis Russo, his tanned, muscular frame relaxed yet alert. Will Wright, his sandy blond hair perfectly messy, stood with Katie Light, her blonde waves cascading over her hourglass figure in a shimmering blue dress.

Raven's lips curved into a sympathetic smile as she opened the envelope in her hand. "The top couples are: Victoria and Xavier, Zack and Claire, and Yolanda and Travis."

A wave of relief washed over the mentioned couples, Victoria and Xavier sharing a triumphant smile, Zack pulling Claire into a brief but tight embrace, and Yolanda and Travis high-fiving each other. The tension in the room eased slightly, but for those not called, the anxiety only intensified.

"Now, for the bottom two," Raven continued, her voice steady but her eyes betraying a flicker of emotion. "Will and Katie, and Matthew and Sammy, please step forward."

Sammy's heart sank as she took Matthew's hand, their fingers intertwining tightly. They stepped forward, their faces masks of trepidation. Will and Katie joined them, Katie's bright blue eyes wide with worry, her southern accent thick as she whispered, "Oh Lord, I hope we're okay."

Raven took a deep breath, her dramatic pause stretching the tension thinner. "The couple leaving the villa is... Matthew and Sammy."

The words hit like a physical blow, the impact reverberating through the room. Sammy's eyes widened, her grip on Matthew's hand tightening as if to anchor herself to him, to their fleeting moment of connection. Matthew's expression was a mix of shock and sorrow, his deep southern accent thick as he whispered, "I thought... I thought we had a chance."

The other contestants were equally stunned, their reactions a chorus of gasps and murmurs. Claire's hand flew to her mouth, her eyes welling up with tears. Zack's jaw clenched, his frustration evident. Victoria and Xavier exchanged a look of disbelief, while Yolanda and Travis seemed torn between relief and sympathy.

As Sammy and Matthew began their walk of shame, their hands still entwined, the weight of their unspoken words hung heavy between them. Sammy's mind raced, her thoughts a chaotic whirlwind. How could this be happening? We were just starting to figure things out. What does this mean for us?

Matthew, his heart aching with a mix of emotions, felt a surge of protectiveness towards Sammy. He wanted to shield her from the pain, to somehow reverse the decision, but he knew it was futile. "We'll figure this out, Sammy," he said, his voice steady despite the turmoil within. "Whatever happens, we'll face it together."

Their exit from the villa was a blur of emotions and goodbyes. Claire pulled Sammy into a tight hug, her tears mingling with Sammy's. "You two are meant to be," she whispered. "Don't let this be the end."

Zack, his arm around Matthew's shoulders, offered a bro-hug and a few words of wisdom. "Sometimes, these things happen for a reason, man. Maybe it's a test, a chance for you to prove that what you have is real."

Victoria, her usual bombshell demeanor softened, approached Sammy with a gentle smile. "You're stronger than you think, Sammy. Don't let this break you."

Yolanda, her bold lips pressed into a sympathetic line, added, "You've got this, girl. Whatever you decide, we're here for you."

As they stepped out of the villa, the warm Hawaiian breeze brushing against their skin, Sammy and Matthew found themselves alone, their hands still clasped, their hearts still intertwined. The future stretched before them, uncertain and daunting, yet filled with possibilities.

"What now?" Sammy asked, her voice small but determined. "Do we... do we try to make this work, or do we accept that this was just a fleeting moment?"

Matthew's gaze intensified, his heart laid bare. "We fight, Sammy. We fight for what we have, for what we could be. I'm not ready to let this go, not without a fight."

Sammy's eyes searched his, her own determination mirroring his. "Then let's fight. Let's show the world, and ourselves, that what we have is real. That it's worth more than a reality show vote."

Hand in hand, they walked away from the villa, their backs straight, their heads held high. The path ahead was uncertain, but together, they were ready to face whatever came their way.

Chapter 12

The days following her elimination from Hot Island had stretched endlessly for Sammy Rodriguez, each hour a labyrinth of doubt and longing. Back in her Houston apartment, the silence was deafening, punctuated only by the hum of the refrigerator and the occasional distant honk of a car. She'd tried to fill the void—nights out with friends, endless scrolling through social media, even a half-hearted attempt at online dating—but nothing could silence the questions swirling in her mind. Had what she felt for Matthew been genuine, or just a carefully curated performance for the cameras? The uncertainty gnawed at her, a persistent ache she couldn't shake.

Her phone buzzed incessantly with messages from friends, family, and fans, all asking the same questions: What happened? Are you okay? What's next? But Sammy's thoughts were elsewhere, fixated on Matthew Brown. His tall, lanky frame, his deep southern drawl, and the way his shy smile had made her heart skip a beat—these memories clung to her like a second skin. She'd replayed their moments together in her mind a thousand times: the stolen glances across the villa, the whispered conversations under the stars, the electric touch of his hand on hers. Yet, the abrupt end to their time on the show had left her feeling robbed, as if their story had been cut short before it could truly begin.

One evening, as she sat on her couch scrolling through old photos from the villa, there was a knock at her door. Her heart leapt into her throat as she peered through the peephole. There he was, Matthew, his curly hair slightly disheveled, a duffel bag slung over his shoulder. Her hand hovered over the doorknob, her pulse racing. What was he doing here? Had he come to say goodbye, or was there a chance—however slim—that he'd come for her?

She swung the door open, the cool evening air carrying the faint scent of rain. "Matthew," she breathed, her voice catching in her throat.

"Hey, Sammy," he said, his voice soft but steady, his deep southern accent wrapping around her like a warm blanket. "Can we talk?"

She stepped aside, letting him in. The apartment felt suddenly smaller, charged with the weight of unspoken words and unfulfilled desires. Matthew set his bag down by the door and turned to face her, his eyes searching hers as if trying to read the depths of her soul.

"I've been thinking about you," he admitted, his gaze intense. "Every day since we left the villa. I couldn't stop wondering if what we had was real, or if it was just... for the show."

Sammy's heart pounded in her chest, a mix of hope and fear warring within her. She wanted to believe him, to trust that what they'd shared was more than just a fleeting connection manufactured for ratings. But the sting of elimination still lingered, a bitter aftertaste that made her hesitant to open herself up again.

"I've been thinking about you too," she confessed, her voice barely above a whisper. "But I don't know, Matthew. It all ended so fast. I didn't get a chance to figure out what we were."

He took a step closer, his presence filling the space between them. "That's why I'm here," he said, his voice firm yet tender. "I don't want it to end like that. I want to know if what I felt was real. If what you felt was real."

Sammy's breath hitched as he closed the distance between them, his hands cupping her face with a gentleness that made her knees weak. His touch was reverent, as if he was afraid she might disappear if he held her too tightly. She felt a surge of longing, a hunger she'd tried to ignore since leaving the villa.

"I missed you," he murmured, his lips brushing against hers in a kiss that was both tentative and hungry.

"I missed you too," she whispered back, her hands finding his shoulders, pulling him closer. The kiss deepened, their lips moving in sync as if they'd been practicing for this moment all along. Sammy's fingers tangled in his hair, her body pressing against his, craving the connection they'd both been denied.

Matthew's hands slid down her back, pulling her tighter against him. She could feel the heat of his body through his shirt, the strength of his muscles beneath her fingertips. It was as if all the doubts and insecurities melted away in that moment, leaving only the raw, undeniable chemistry between them.

"I love you, Sammy," he said, his breath hot against her ear, his voice thick with emotion. "I know it's crazy, but I do. I've never felt this way about anyone before."

Her heart swelled at his words, a mix of relief and joy washing over her. "I love you too," she confessed, her voice trembling. "I was so scared it was all just... pretend."

"It wasn't," he assured her, his lips trailing down her neck, sending shivers down her spine. "This is real. We're real."

Sammy's hands moved to the hem of his shirt, pulling it over his head and tossing it aside. His chest was lean and sculpted, his skin warm and golden under the soft glow of the apartment lights. She traced her fingers over the freckles scattered across his shoulders, marveling at the contrast of his light brown skin against her olive tone.

Matthew's hands moved to the zipper of her dress, slowly pulling it down, revealing the curve of her busty figure. The dress fell to the floor, leaving her in nothing but her lace lingerie. His gaze raked over her, hungry and appreciative, making her feel desired in a way she hadn't before.

"You're so fucking beautiful," he murmured, his hands cupping her breasts, his thumbs brushing over her nipples. "I've thought about touching you every single day."

Sammy moaned softly, arching into his touch. "Matthew," she breathed, her head falling back as he kissed his way down her chest, his lips and tongue leaving a trail of fire in their wake. She guided him back to the couch, pushing him down gently and straddling his lap. His hands gripped her hips, his eyes dark with desire as she ground against him, feeling the hardness of his erection through his jeans.

"I want you," she whispered, her hands moving to the button of his pants, unfastening them with trembling fingers. "Now."

Matthew groaned as she pulled his pants and boxers down, his thick, throbbing cock springing free. She took a moment to admire him, her fingers wrapping around his shaft, stroking him slowly. He hissed at the contact, his head falling back against the couch.

"Fuck, Sammy," he groaned. "You're gonna make me lose it."

She smiled, leaning down to kiss him, her lips brushing against his as she guided him inside her. He filled her completely, stretching her in a way that made her gasp, her nails digging into his shoulders.

"You feel so good," he murmured, his hands gripping her hips as he began to move, thrusting upward in a slow, deliberate rhythm. "So tight, so wet... fuck, Sammy."

Sammy moaned, her body moving in sync with his, her breasts bouncing with each thrust. The couch creaked beneath them, the sounds of their passion filling the room. She could feel the tension building, a coil tightening in her core as Matthew's pace quickened, his movements becoming more urgent.

"Harder," she panted, her hands gripping his shoulders. "I need you harder, Matthew. Fuck me like you've been dreaming about."

Matthew growled, his hands sliding down to her ass, lifting her as he pounded into her with relentless force. The pleasure was overwhelming, a tidal wave crashing over her as she cried out, her body trembling on the edge of release.

"Matthew, I'm close," she gasped, her voice hoarse. "Don't stop, don't you fucking stop."

"Me too," he groaned, his thrusts becoming frantic. "Come with me, Sammy. Let go, baby. Let me feel you fall apart."

His words pushed her over the edge, her orgasm ripping through her like a storm, her body convulsing as she screamed his name.

Matthew followed moments later, his hips stuttering as he filled her, his deep groan vibrating against her chest.

They stayed like that for a moment, breathless and entwined, before Matthew gently pulled out and laid her down on the couch, his arms wrapping around her. Sammy rested her head on his chest, listening to the steady beat of his heart, feeling the warmth of his skin against hers.

"That was... incredible," she murmured, her fingers tracing patterns on his chest. "I've never felt anything like that."

"Yeah," he agreed, his voice thick with emotion. "It was everything I'd hoped for and more."

They lay there in silence for a while, the only sound the soft hum of the air conditioner and the distant murmur of the city outside. Sammy felt a sense of peace she hadn't experienced in weeks, a feeling of rightness that she couldn't deny. But as the initial rush of passion faded, the weight of their situation settled back into her mind.

"What now?" she asked, breaking the silence. "Do we... try to make this work? Without the cameras, I mean."

Matthew propped himself up on one elbow, his gaze searching hers. "I want to," he said, his voice firm. "I want to see where this goes. I don't want to let you go, Sammy. Not again."

She smiled, reaching up to brush a strand of hair from his face. "Me neither," she admitted. "But it's not going to be easy. We're from such different worlds. You're a farmer from Snow Hill, and I'm a city girl from Houston. We have different lives, different expectations."

"I know," he said, his hand covering hers. "But I'm willing to figure it out. If you are. I'm not afraid of hard work, Sammy. And if loving you means bridging the gap between our worlds, then that's what I'll do."

Sammy nodded, her heart swelling with hope. "I am," she said, her voice steady. "Let's do this. Let's see where it takes us."

Matthew leaned down, pressing a soft kiss to her lips. "Together," he whispered. "Always together."

As they lay there, wrapped in each other's arms, Sammy felt a sense of possibility she hadn't felt in a long time. The future was uncertain, but for the first time, she wasn't afraid. With Matthew by her side, she knew they could face anything.

Later that night, as they cooked dinner together in her small kitchen, the ease of their interaction surprised her. Matthew chopped vegetables with a skill that spoke of years of practice, while Sammy seasoned the meat, their movements synchronized as if they'd been doing this for years. The conversation flowed naturally, touching on everything from their childhoods to their dreams for the future.

"You're going to make it happen," he said, his voice filled with confidence. "I can see it already."

"Thanks," she replied, her cheeks flushing with warmth. "It means a lot to hear you say that."

As they ate, the laughter and easy banter continued, the tension of their earlier conversation replaced by a comfortable silence that spoke volumes. Afterward, they curled up on the couch, a blanket draped over their legs, watching a movie neither of them paid much attention to. Sammy's head rested on Matthew's shoulder, his arm wrapped securely around her.

"This feels right," she murmured, her eyes half-closed.

"It does," he agreed, pressing a kiss to the top of her head. "Feels like home."

In that moment, Sammy knew she'd made the right choice. The road ahead wouldn't be easy, but with Matthew by her side, she was ready to face whatever came their way. Their love was real, and it was worth fighting for.

Chapter 13

Months had passed since Sammy Rodriguez and Matthew Brown left the villa, their hearts forever intertwined in a bond that had only deepened with time. The chaos of Hot Island felt like a distant memory, replaced by the quiet rhythms of everyday life. Sammy had settled into her apartment in Houston, but her thoughts often wandered to Matthew, the man who had captured her heart with his quiet charm and unwavering loyalty. Despite their different worlds—Sammy's bustling city life and Matthew's serene farm in Snow Hill—they had found a way to bridge the gap, their love a testament to the power of connection.

One crisp autumn morning, as the first hints of frost kissed the air, Sammy received a call from Matthew. His deep southern drawl filled her ears, and her heart skipped a beat. "Hey, Sammy," he said, his voice warm and familiar, like a favorite blanket on a cold night. "I've been thinkin'. I want you to come live with me in Snow Hill. For real this time. No cameras, no drama. Just us."

Sammy's breath caught in her throat. She had always been drawn to the idea of a simpler life, one that contrasted sharply with the noise and chaos of her city existence. The thought of waking up to the sound of roosters crowing and the sight of endless fields was both terrifying and exhilarating. "Are you serious?" she asked, her voice trembling with a mix of excitement and uncertainty.

"Dead serious," Matthew replied, his tone leaving no room for doubt. "I know it's a big change, but I think you'll love it here. The farm, the fresh air, the peace... and me, of course." His words were like a promise, a lifeline pulling her toward a future she hadn't dared to imagine.

Sammy laughed, a sound that bubbled up from deep within her chest. Her heart swelled with joy, and she felt a surge of courage she hadn't known she possessed. "I'd love to, Matthew. I really would."

True to his word, Matthew arrived in Houston a week later, his truck packed with her belongings. As they drove away from the city, Sammy felt a sense of anticipation she hadn't experienced in years. The skyscrapers gave way to open fields, the concrete jungle melting into a patchwork of green and brown. The air grew crisp and clean, carrying the scent of earth and pine. By the time they reached Snow Hill, Sammy was already enchanted by the rolling hills and the slow pace of life.

Matthew's farm was everything she had imagined and more. The house, a weathered but sturdy structure with a wraparound porch, sat nestled among acres of cornfields and a small barn where chickens clucked contentedly. The air smelled of hay and woodsmoke, and the silence was broken only by the occasional call of a distant bird. Matthew introduced her to his parents, who welcomed her with open arms and warm smiles. For the first time, Sammy felt like she belonged somewhere outside of her own family.

Days turned into weeks, and Sammy settled into the rhythm of farm life. She woke up before dawn, the chill of the morning air a stark contrast to the warmth of her bed. Matthew taught her how to milk the cows, their large brown eyes watching her curiously as she fumbled with the milking stool. She learned to ride horses, her thighs aching from the unfamiliar motion, but the sense of freedom as she galloped across the fields was worth every moment of discomfort. The hard work was rewarding, and the quiet moments with Matthew were priceless.

One sunny afternoon, as the golden light of late autumn bathed the fields in a warm glow, Matthew surprised Sammy with a horseback ride. He led her to the stables, where a beautiful chestnut mare awaited. "Her name's Belle. I purchased her just for you," he said.

"Really?" Sammy asked. Sammy couldn't help but to smile as she stared at Matthew in this cowboy hat, jeans and shirt. She too dressed in a cowboy hat, jeans and blouse.

Matthew nodded. "I know how much you love riding and I wanted you go have a horse for your own." He smiled, his hands steady as he helped Sammy into the saddle. "She's gentle, just like you. I have one more surprise for you too. Follow me."

He grabbed a black haired mare and throw his leg over the saddled. With a subtle kick and a whistle, the horse galloped out of the barn towards the open flat plain, followed by Sammy's horse.

They rode through the fields, the wind rustling through Sammy's long dark hair as they laughed and talked. The sun was high in the sky, casting a golden glow over the landscape. Matthew guided them to an open area near a small grove of trees, where a picnic blanket was spread out, laden with food and a bottle of wine. A checkered tablecloth fluttered in the breeze, and the scent of fresh bread and cheese wafted through the air.

"What's all this?" Sammy asked, her eyes widening in delight. The setup was straight out of a fairy tale, and she felt like the luckiest woman in the world.

Matthew grinned, his eyes sparkling with mischief. His scruffy beard caught the light, and his freckles stood out against his light brown skin. "Just a little something I put together. Thought we could enjoy the day together."

They dismounted their horse and tied them to an nearby tree. Taking her hand, Matthew let her to the blanket, and they sat on the ground, sharing a meal of sandwiches, fresh fruit, and cheese. Matthew poured the wine, the deep red liquid glinting in the sunlight as they clinked glasses. "To us," he said, his voice soft but full of meaning.

"To us," Sammy echoed, her heart swelling with happiness. As they ate, she felt a sense of contentment she had never known before. This was it—this was happiness. The simplicity of the moment, the warmth of Matthew's presence, and the beauty of the surrounding nature all combined to create a perfect bubble of joy.

After the meal, Matthew grew serious. He took Sammy's hand in his, his thumb brushing gently over her skin. His touch sent shivers down her spine, and she felt her heart race with anticipation. "Sammy," he began, his voice soft but steady, like the rumble of distant thunder. "I've been thinkin' a lot about us. About what we have, and what I want for our future."

Sammy's breath caught in her throat as she met his gaze. His eyes, deep pools of brown, held an intensity that made her stomach flutter. "What do you mean, Matthew?"

He reached into his pocket and pulled out a small velvet box. Opening it, he revealed a simple yet elegant diamond ring. The sunlight caught the stone, sending sparks of light dancing across the blanket. "Sammy Rodriguez, we may have lost Hot Island and the prize of $250,000, but I won the best prizes on earth, *you*."" he said, his voice filled with emotion, "that said, Sammy would you make me the happiest man on Earth? Will you marry me? Will you be my wife, and spend the rest of your life with me here in Snow Hill?"

Tears welled up in Sammy's eyes as she nodded, unable to speak. Her throat was tight with emotion, and her heart felt like it might burst from her chest. Matthew slipped the ring onto her finger, the cool metal a stark contrast to the warmth of his touch. She threw her arms around him, kissing him passionately. "Yes, Matthew," she whispered against his lips. "Yes, a thousand times yes."

The moment was perfect, but neither of them was content to let it end there. As they pulled apart, Matthew's eyes darkened with desire, and Sammy felt her own hunger stirring. The air between them crackled with tension, and she could feel the heat radiating from his body. "I love you, Sammy," he murmured, his lips brushing against hers. "And I want to show you just how much."

Without another word, he laid her down on the picnic blanket, his hands roaming over her body with a familiarity that sent shivers down her spine. Sammy's heart pounded as she reached for him, her fingers tracing the contours of his muscular frame. The air was warm, the grass soft beneath them, and the world seemed to fade away as they lost themselves in each other.

Matthew's lips trailed down her neck, his breath hot against her skin. "You're so fucking beautiful," he whispered, his hands cupping her breasts, his thumbs teasing her nipples until they pebbled with desire. Sammy moaned, arching her back as he kissed his way down her body, his mouth leaving a trail of fire in its wake. Her curves, accentuated by her form-fitting jeans, seemed to beckon him closer, and he answered the call with eager hands and hungry lips.

She tugged at his shirt, desperate to feel his skin against hers. Matthew obliged, shedding his clothes with practiced ease. His body was lean and strong, his skin warm and inviting. Sammy ran her hands over his chest, her fingers tangling in his curly hair as he kissed her deeply, their tongues entwining in a dance as old as time. His scruffy beard scratched her skin in the most delightful way, and she couldn't help but moan into his mouth.

Matthew's hands moved lower, slipping beneath her jeans to cup her ass, lifting her hips as he pressed against her, his erection thick and insistent. Sammy gasped, her nails digging into his shoulders as he teased her, his fingers brushing against her core, already wet with anticipation. "Matthew, please," she pleaded, her voice thick with need. Her body was on fire, every nerve ending screaming for him.

He smiled against her skin, his eyes dark with desire. "Anything for you, Sammy."

With a swift motion, he shed the rest of her clothes, leaving her bare beneath the open sky. The sun warmed her skin, and the breeze played over her body, heightening every sensation. Her olive skin glowed in the sunlight, and her beauty mark above her left eyebrow seemed to pulse with life. Matthew's lips found hers again, his kisses hungry and demanding as he positioned himself between her legs.

Sammy wrapped her legs around his waist, pulling him closer as he entered her with a slow, deliberate thrust. She gasped at the sensation, her body stretching to accommodate him, her walls clenching around his thickness. Matthew groaned, his forehead resting against hers as he began to move, his hips rocking in a steady rhythm that sent waves of pleasure crashing over her. The feeling of him filling her was indescribable, and she knew in that moment that she was exactly where she was meant to be.

The world around them seemed to dissolve, leaving only the two of them, their bodies moving in perfect harmony. Matthew's hands gripped her hips, guiding her as he thrust deeper, his breath coming in ragged gasps. Sammy met his rhythm, her body arching to meet his, her cries of pleasure echoing across the field. Him taking her in the open was primal and sensual. Only the birds and bees could be heard as they fucked loudly. The grass tickled her back, and the sun warmed her skin, but all she could focus on was the man above her, the man who had claimed her heart and her body.

"I love you, Sammy," Matthew murmured, his voice hoarse with emotion as he pummeled into her. "I'll always love you."

"I love you too," she replied, her voice trembling as the pleasure built, spiraling tighter and tighter until she could no longer hold back. Her body shook as she climaxed, her walls tightening around him, milking him as she cried out his name. The orgasm ripped through her, a tidal wave of sensation that left her breathless and trembling.

Matthew followed soon after, his body stiffening as he buried himself deep within her, his release hot and intense. He collapsed onto her, his weight pressing her into the blanket, his heart pounding against hers. For a long moment, they lay there, their naked sweaty bodies still joined, their breaths slowly returning to normal. The world was silent except for the sound of their ragged breathing and the distant call of a bird.

Matthew kissed her forehead, his lips soft and tender. "You're my everything, Sammy," he whispered. "My wife, my partner, my forever."

Sammy smiled, her heart overflowing with love. "And you're mine, Matthew. Always and forever."

As the sun dipped lower in the sky, casting a golden glow over the field, they dressed and packed up the picnic, their hearts full and their bodies sated. Hand in hand, they walked back to the farm, the promise of a lifetime together stretching out before them like the endless horizon. The air was cool, but the warmth of their love kept them comfortable.

In the months that followed, Sammy and Matthew built a life together in Snow Hill, their love growing stronger with each passing day. They married in a small, intimate ceremony surrounded by family and friends. The vows they exchanged were a testament to the bond they had forged, a bond that had been tested and strengthened by time and distance. Sammy wore a simple yet elegant dress, her long dark hair styled in loose waves that cascaded down her back. Matthew looked dashing in a suit, his scruffy beard and curly hair giving him a rugged charm that made her heart skip a beat.

As they danced under the stars, the night air filled with the scent of blooming flowers and the sound of laughter, Sammy knew that she had found her happily ever after—not just in Matthew's arms, but in the quiet, simple life they had built together. Their love story, born on the chaotic shores of Hot Island, had found its true home in the peaceful fields of Snow Hill. And as they looked to the future, hand in hand, they knew that their journey was only just beginning.

The days blended into weeks, and the weeks into months, each one a testament to the strength of their love. They faced challenges, of course—the unpredictability of the farm, the long hours of work, and the occasional disagreement—but they faced them together, their bond unshakable. Sammy learned to cook hearty meals that fueled Matthew after long days in the fields, and he surprised her with small tokens of his love, like wildflowers picked from the meadow or a spontaneous dance in the kitchen.

Their love was not just in the grand gestures, but in the everyday moments—the way Matthew's eyes lit up when she walked into the room, the way Sammy's laughter filled the house, the way they held hands as they watched the sunset over the fields. It was in the quiet conversations by the fireplace, the shared dreams of the future, and the unspoken understanding that they were each other's forever.

In the end, it was not the grand adventures or the wild nights that defined their love, but the quiet moments, the shared laughter, and the unwavering commitment to each other. And as they stood on the porch of their farmhouse, watching the sun set over the fields they had built a life on, Sammy knew that she had found her happily ever after—in Matthew's arms, in the heart of Snow Hill, and in the love that would last a lifetime.

Don't miss out!

Visit the website below and you can sign up to receive emails whenever Michael Gordon publishes a new book. There's no charge and no obligation.

https://books2read.com/r/B-A-KEXRC-ECCKG

Did you love *A Reality TV Romance*? Then you should read *Will You Marry Me?*[1] by Michael Gordon!

[2]

The sun-kissed shores of Virginia Beach played host to a unique social experiment, a reality TV show that aimed to bring two strangers together in the hope of finding love. Among the eager participants were Zayden Moss, a charismatic former athlete, and Sabrina Chun, a reserved nurse with a rebellious streak. Their paths were about to collide in the most unexpected way, and the cameras were there to capture every moment. In the end of the experiment, will they stay married or be divorced? Find out in this season of Will you Marry Me?

---

1. https://books2read.com/u/4AlJdk

2. https://books2read.com/u/4AlJdk

Also by Michael Gordon

Will You Marry Me?
Love & War: The Battle of Virginia Beach
Forbidden Freedom
The Geek's Dating Coach
A Love in Two Lands
A Reality TV Romance

About the Author

Michael Gordon is a modern romance author who enjoys writing steamy, heart racing, interracial romances. When he's not writing, he's reading other swoon worthy interracial romance stories, traveling with his wife & kids, or watching sports. He also writes Sci-Fi and Fantasy under his other pen name, Matthew Gage.